Moonshadows

A Novel of the Far North

Robert B. Gregg

Avalon House Classics

I wish to express my heartfelt thanks to my wife, Nancy, whose devotion, encouragement, and excellent editing constituted a tremendous contribution to this novel.

This book is dedicated to the thousands of fishermen who fly every year into Northern Canada in search of the wilderness and adventure.

Copyright © 2016 Robert B. Gregg

All Rights Reserved

ISBN-13: 978-1511416245

ISBN-10: 1511416246

Prologue

We've come back to the place where the tragedy happened, and as I write the final words to this story, in my memory are wounds that won't heal.

Night has fallen. In front of the cabin, under the light of a full moon, the Albany River flows swiftly on its way to Hudson Bay.

Outside, the campfire burns bright and the orange flames, trimmed in yellow, leap up and disappear into the black, starlit sky.

I sit inside at the table and compose this narrative in tribute to the dead and those who sacrificed some part of their spirit to the wild Canadian North.

I tremble in fear from the evil I witnessed, for deep within me is a remembrance so graphically clear it touches my soul.

This is a difficult story to recount because it brings sad memories.

A warm breeze sways the branches of the trees and their shadows dance across the grass near the cabin door.

The survivors gather round the blaze. I am about to join them. We will lift our glasses once more in salute to the departed.

We miss them, but they are always with us.

We see their faces every day.

Robert B. Gregg

Chapter 1

Sitting behind his desk in a high-backed leather chair in downtown Detroit, Tom Sullivan removed a cigar from the humidor in front of him.

Looking at it carefully, he lined up the Arturo Fuente Hemingway with one eye and cut it cleanly.

He flipped on his butane lighter and rotated the blunt end in the flame. Placing the cigar in his mouth, he slowly rotated it and gently took a draw.

The procedure done, he leaned back in his chair, and blew two perfect circles of smoke that lifted gently to the ceiling and disappeared. He seemed satisfied.

The plan was firm. The annual fishing expedition was finalized. The group would leave in a few days.

Tom smiled at the four of us, tilted his head, drew in the smoke, and blew a fist-sized circle that drifted slowly upwards and softly faded away on the ceiling.

He appeared to achieve some inner joy from watching the floating exhales. He leaned forward across his desk.

"We've always wanted to go back, gentlemen," he said. "Well, the mighty Albany River is about to see the likes of us again. Are you ready?"

Victor and I let out an enthusiastic, "Absolutely."

"The Albany. I can't wait," added Charlie, Tom's brother-in-law, and a newcomer to the group.

Sloan Jankowski just smiled and nodded his approval.

Our thoughts were on the Albany.

Tom was of average height with dark brown hair he wouldn't allow to turn gray. He liked superior wines, especially from the Rombauer Vineyard in California, and fine cigars.

Quiet and well organized, over the years we gained confidence in his leadership. Tom didn't ask to be our leader, we just somehow appointed him to the task. He booked the outfitter, hired the guide, bought the groceries and made sure each of the expedition's members possessed the essentials so we would not be a burden on one another.

When he set out to do something, he did it well. Tom studied fishing, and if anyone could be called an expert, in a sport where there are no experts, he had obtained that status through his skills.

He was a high school football star in Rochester Hills and won a scholarship to the University of Michigan. He was a place-kicker for the Wolverines, and a 3200-meter runner on the track team.

Tom notched a couple of game-winning field goals in his career, but now, past 50, he was no longer an athlete.

After college, Tom went on to build a publishing empire, including daily and weekly newspapers in Michigan, and a magazine for snowbirds in Orlando, Florida. He is one of the most successful men I know.

A simple, but dapper dresser, Tom wore a plain black suit, white shirt and a tie with earth tone designs made up of hieroglyphics copied from the wall of a Pharaoh's tomb.

He once told me, "Mike. When you go to a meeting no one remembers what kind of suit you're wearing. The only thing they remember is your tie. Always wear a knockout tie."

He was right.

We came to the final planning session straight from work. All of us wore suits and ties, except Charlie Watson. Dressed in jeans, he wore a tie-dyed T-shirt covered by a well-worn Orvis fishing vest. He would be a hippie forever.

We felt excitement in the air. Often I thought the sheer anticipation of an expedition, and the numerous conversations leading up to going, became a big part of the adventure.

"To the Albany River and great friendship!" Tom said, rising from his chair and lifting his glass of single-malt Scotch in a toast.

"To the Albany and fun," toasted Charlie.

"To the Albany," saluted Victor and Sloan.

"To the Albany," I chimed in.

Our liquid salute wasn't a pledge to the river itself, but to one another. It was promise to put our fellowship first, and our egos second.

I admired Tom ever since we met on a fishing expedition 25 years ago. He is someone you would trust with your life.

Standing together, we all gazed out of his office window toward Comerica Park, the Detroit Tiger's stadium. It was early May and a heavy spring shower attempted to clean the decaying city.

Our thoughts were back in the Canadian wilds fishing the Albany River. In our minds we waded the river's back eddies and cast for trophy fish. The Albany is full of walleye, northern pike, whitefish and some of the biggest brook trout on this planet. The river is vast, and complete with whitewater rapids, waterfalls, and danger.

For thousands of years the Indians relied on the Albany as a water route that took them from Lake Superior to Hudson Bay via Lake Nipigon and the Nipigon River. Archeologists have found evidence that the same Natives traded as far as the Atlantic coast.

In the 1600's, the Indians shared their knowledge of the routes with fur traders and explorers, and what is known today as Canada, opened up to the world.

Years ago, The Hudson Bay Company controlled the Albany, and the rest of Canada for that matter. The company shipped thousands upon thousands of beaver pelts down the river in freighter canoes headed for Fort Albany, the firm's post on Hudson Bay. From there they were shipped to Europe.

Today, the Albany remains a wilderness river used only by Indians and adventurous fishermen.

"Ray Olson will fly us in," Tom said. "I have already talked to him.

"We leave Detroit early on Sunday, June 1st. We spend the first night, as usual, in Sault Saint Marie, Canada, at the Watertower Inn and, the next day, we'll drive through to Nakina. We fly in at dawn on Tuesday, June 3rd."

"Did you make reservations in the Sault and Nakina?" I asked.

"Yes," he said, as he turned to his desk and unrolled a Canadian Government map of the Albany River area. "I'll email a copy of our itinerary to everyone."

We gathered around him.

"This will be the fifth trip to the Albany for everyone except Charlie," Tom said. "This is his first."

Tom took the cigar out of his mouth, put on his reading glasses, and pointed at the map, "These jagged lines signify a waterfall, Charlie. In high water the falls are a dangerous place. You see this rocky point?"

"Yes."

"This is where Mike and Victor almost lost their lives three years ago. Tell him the story, Mike."

"We were on our way back to the cabin after a day of fishing. Our guide Grey Wolf, Tom, and Sloan had already portaged the falls and were waiting for Victor and me above the rapids.

"We were doing everything right, but sometimes that's not enough. We had finished the portage. Standing in the shallows above the falls, I held the boat steady while Victor started the engine. We always made sure it was running smooth before we ran up the rapids.

"Victor cranked the engine and the motor hummed. He signaled me to board, and I crawled over the side. We maneuvered into the whitewater and everything looked good, then the engine cut out. We started drifting backwards in the fast current. The rapids took hold of us. We headed towards the precipice of the falls. I yelled at Victor to crank, and he yanked the cord like a madman, but the engine failed to start.

"The falls were coming fast, so I curled up in the bow, ready to go over when, at the last possible moment, the engine started.

"We hung in the trough of the last wave about to go over the falls. The boat seemed to stay on the lip of the cataract forever, then the prop caught the water and we surged upstream. Victor kept the motor at full speed and we shot right past Grey Wolf."

"We were already talking about what we would have to do to rescue them," explained Tom.

"Victor never slowed down," I continued. "He ran the throttle full open all the way to the cabin. Neither of us said a word. When we approached the shore, Victor didn't use the dock, he ran the boat full-speed onto the gravel beach.

I lurched forward and fell to the bottom of the boat, when Victor shouted to me, 'I could use a drink. How about you?'

"Without a doubt, the most exciting moment of my life."

"Mine too," agreed Victor.

"Jesus," said Charlie. "You guys are scaring me."

The rest of us smiled at the memory.

The fellowship and conversation in Tom's office heightened our anticipation.

We traveled north every year not just for fish, the trip gave us time to think about our lives, time to commit to us, our friendship and, at the same time, it gave us the solitude so lacking in our lives.

Over the years, we returned to the vastness and silence of the North to escape from civilization. An annual challenge to understand if we could still handle the best nature had to offer. You are never in control, no matter what the plan or preparation. The wilderness calls the shots. You accept the challenges, and try to have fun meeting every one.

Every accomplishment is a good feeling, and every trip North is a reward in itself. This one would be no different. We knew in advance we would be rewarded.

In the Far North you are dependent on your own resourcefulness. You take what nature dishes out and try to take advantage of each opportunity. The wilderness, however, has a way of humbling the proud.

I went to fish. I didn't always catch fish, but I vowed to give it my best shot.

I used to consider fishing a competition of sorts, me against the fish, however, I have completed the transition, and now regard myself an angler who just plain loves to be in the beautiful places where fish are found.

"What is the weather like?" Charlie inquired.

"It might be 60 degrees or it could snow," Tom explained, "anything can happen. Dress in layers. By the way, the winter snowfall dictates how high the spring flow will be on the river."

Gourmet food is Charlie's specialty we would eat like kings. He baked, broiled, grilled, poached and fried with the best of them.

The last of the hippies, Charlie attended the original Woodstock, and the reunion years later. A union negotiator for the UAW at the Ford Plant in River Rouge, Charlie was as liberal as they come, even though he refused to admit to being one. He called himself a "Progressive."

A tall, balding, lanky fellow with a shaggy beard taking up most of his face, he had an aversion to "anyone who makes a lot of money" and Richard Nixon.

Charlie came from a wealthy family and the rest of us always thought that he felt guilty about his background.

He is a lovable character, however, always pleasant and possesses a nonchalant sense of humor. No one is safe from his jokes, and the only problem is that he told the same ones over and over.

Next to me is Victor Putnam, an attorney and whiskey connoisseur, who smokes expensive cigars. An agreeable and witty fellow, he is a tall, good-looking man with a penchant for being well dressed and "different."

Victor loved Jack Daniels and was a former Captain in the Army who fought in Afghanistan after our tour in Iraq. He still worked out on a regular basis and possessed a beard much like Charlie's, only well kempt.

"This trip sounds more adventurous than usual," said Victor, "but I like the itinerary, Tom. If this is half the fun as last time, we'll have a blast."

"As long as we're ready," said Tom. "Say Victor, you've lost some weight?"

"I have," said Victor, patting his firm stomach. "Twenty pounds so far. I've been canoeing the river by my house three or four days a week to prepare; I love it."

"I'm proud of you," Sloan told Victor. "I've always been interested in canoeing, but between running and tennis, I just don't have the time."

Sloan is a neurosurgeon. The best. He is also the one true woodsman among us. He can paddle canoe, chop wood, portage and out-hike the rest of us. Sloan had one drawback, he was afraid of the dark, a common fear called achluophobia.

I liked going north with him, because having a doctor along is very reassuring.

Sloan confessed to an offbeat background. A pilot, he twice ran guns to rebel groups in South America to put himself through medical school, and he had also worked as a demolition expert for a company that brought down buildings.

"Yea," he once told us sarcastically, "those jobs really prepared me for life as a physician."

Years ago, Sloan stood on the runways in places like Venezuela and Columbia and traded cases of guns for money with strangers.

"Those were some touchy moments," he told us. "They might just as easily have shot me and taken the weapons, but they didn't."

Now, Sloan is a quiet, affable family man, with a knockout wife named Chloe and two teenage boys, fourteen and sixteen. He has dark blond hair; combed straight back like they did in the 50's, and his bright green eyes gazed into your soul when you talked to him. His jaw was square, and he was always clean-shaven, even in the wilderness. His face was toughened by years spent in the outdoors.

"Are we going to hire a guide?" Sloan asked. We usually only hired one if we had never been to the place before, or if we thought the expedition might prove more dangerous than usual.

Tom pondered for a moment, then made up his mind. "Yes," he said. "We could go on our own, we've done it before, but we are going early, and if the water is high we might need help. Better safe than dead. We'll hire Winston again."

Winston "Grey Wolf" Wallace is the best guide on the Albany. He is part of a sizable Cree Indian family that grew up in the region and no one knew the Albany's rapids better than Winston.

Winston's grandfather was a Scottish trapper named William Wallace. The males in his family all had blue eyes. His families were descendants of the Scottish hero William Wallace portrayed by Mel Gibson in the movie "Braveheart."

Victor and I glanced at one another, smiled, and nodded our heads in agreement with the plan.

"That OK with you Sloan?" Tom said.

"Sounds good," he answered. Tom often looked for Sloan's approval.

The decision made, Winston Wallace would be our guide. The expedition to the Albany River was set.

Robert B. Gregg

Chapter 2

We spent the first night in Sault Saint Marie, Canada, after a long drive up Interstate 75 from Detroit. Well into our second day of travel, North of White River, Ontario, we made a right hand turn and traveled several miles and stopped.

A lengthy gravel road stretched before us to the left, snaking its way through the Canadian wilderness. We used this logging road year after year as a shortcut from Trans Canada Highway 17 to Highway 11.

Charlie turned off the pavement onto the gravel. A sign read, "This is a private road. Travel at your own risk." We learned years ago to take this message seriously.

Now we faced the notorious "short cut." The logging road was open to the public, but the warning had to be heeded.

"Hang on guys!" Charlie yelled, his big eyes dominating his long, narrow face and shaggy beard. He stomped on the accelerator and the vehicle launched forward trying hard to achieve traction as tons of gravel rattled off the undercarriage. The van sounded like a cement mixer.

Inside the car we could taste the dust. The vents were closed, but the super fine powder penetrated the vehicle.

We went faster and faster. The Dodge Caravan skidded, the many small stones acting like ball bearings. Rocks flew and nothing could be seen out the back except a cloud of dust constantly following us, blocking out the blue horizon.

The trees off the road stood short. The area had been lumbered in recent years, and the new growth was just a few feet high. A grey-colored dust, thrown into the air by numerous logging trucks, coated the trees. The vehicle was jam-packed with the five of us, fishing gear, duffels and a huge cooler. A smaller cooler along with groceries and additional gear was tied down to a rooftop rack, and two huge rod tubes were strapped to the roof with bungee cords.

We slipped around a wicked corner at high speed. Charlie wore a devilish grin masking the true danger of what he did. Stones flew into the spruce trees and heavy brush of the forest.

"Slow down! I knew I shouldn't have let you drive," said Tom as Charlie hit an enormous chuckhole, catapulting both of them out of their seats, banging Tom's head into the visor.

"Wahoo," shouted the airborne Charlie. "Relax, Tom. We're having fun."

Our trio in the back seat, laughed, and hung on.

"We aren't going to experience fun unless we arrive in Nakina alive," said Tom with an awkward smile. "Be more careful with my vehicle."

The sun appeared over the horizon, and the road ran straighter than before. Charlie picked up speed

Tom hung on, one hand tightly gripping his seat, the other clasped to the handle over the door. We all bounced around.

"Geez," said a laughing Victor. "I don't want to die like this, in the middle of nowhere."

Charlie lifted his foot off the pedal.

"The guys grading the road churned up some monster rocks," he said. "I'll...."

We dropped into a chuckhole the size of our tires and only the tight seat belts kept us from hitting our heads on the roof.

"Wow!" said Charlie. "Sorry Tom." He gained control and concentrated, looking straight ahead. "Isn't this a kick?"

"Better slow down. I've had enough excitement already," said Victor. "I don't remember laughing this hard since last year."

"OK, but the ride won't be as much fun."

"We're going to die," Sloan said jokingly, and laughed hysterically.

Charlie backed off the speed.

We swerved between huge rocks and chuckholes for the next ten miles, bouncing along past clear cuts and stacks of old timber. The logs were cut and stacked into short lengths and piled on the side of the road. The piles of wood were haphazard and covered in a gray dust kicked up by the logging trucks. They were dry and looked like they could easily ignite.

We passed a big open area that had burned five years before. The charred forest went four miles long by road and out of sight on both sides, and look a lot like a giant black scab on the earth.

We all looked at it and the laughter stopped. "Probably caused by some smoker," commented Sloan.

Charlie made another turn and slowed as we headed into the rising sun. "I can't see a thing," he informed us, squinting and ducking under the

Moonshadows

shadow of the visor.

"Why don't you put your sunglasses on?" Tom said. "Sometimes I think you'd rather go blind than wear them. Hell, you don't even use them when you're fishing."

We drove on for several minutes and skidded around a tight right-hand turn, and Tom shouted, "Pull over here!"

Charlie abruptly pulled off the side of the road near a small picturesque stream where we stopped every year.

"I need a beer," Charlie said as he jumped out of the vehicle. He walked around back to the cooler and pulled out a cold can of beer.

"A little early for me," I said when Charlie offered me one, and then my dry throat reminded me how thirsty I was, and how tasty a beer would be after consuming dust for 20 miles.

"Wait," I quickly said as he started to walk away. "I'll have one."

"Here," he said, handing me a can of Molson's Canadian.

"How about you guys?" Charlie said to the others.

"It's not even noon," said Tom.

"Well it's noon somewhere," said Charlie, as he walked back and pulled a cold can of Canadian from the cooler and handed it to Tom.

Sloan and Victor went over to the edge of the brush and took a leak while the rest of us walked down to the bridge over the stream.

"No fish in that creek," Tom advised me.

For ten years I fished the stream every time we stopped. Nothing. This year I wouldn't even try.

Sloan and Victor joined us. Standing on the bridge drinking our beer, we noticed a cloud of dust coming at us from about a mile away. We followed the cloud with our eyes until a truck popped out of it and pulled up next to us. The truck came to a stop and the gray haze of powder continued on and settled on our group.

I covered my beer so the dust wouldn't get in, and as the air cleared, the driver of the beat-up, old Ford pickup rolled down his window and called over to us. "Has youse guys seen any bears?"

We glanced at one another and stared at the driver.

"Bears. You know them furry black animals."

Everyone laughed.

The driver looked at the front of our vehicle and observed there were no plates.

15

"Youse guys must be from the States?"

"Yes sir," said Charlie, beer trickling down his beard.

"Oh, son," said the man in the truck. "Don't be calling me sir. I'm not a fish and wildlife officer. Hell no. I'm Jack Burke, people around here call me 'Canada Jack,' and this is Scott MacIntosh. We're out hunting for bear, or anything else we can shoot and eat."

His voice seemed friendly. The kind of voice you liked to hear from a stranger in the wild.

"Want a beer?" Charlie said, never a stranger long.

"Sure," the pair said simultaneously.

"Isn't spring bear season closed?" Victor asked.

"Hell ya," said Canada Jack, "but closures don't mean shit to us."

"Those idiot PETA people in Toronto put pressure on the provincial parliament and they called off the spring bear hunt a few years back," he added.

He got out and accepted a beer from Charlie.

Jack was short, stout and had a pale, oval face. He looked like he suffered an illness, or, more likely, a hangover.

His buddy Scott emerged and Tom handed him a Molson's. Scott stood tall, thin in build, and his eyes were in a fixed stare as if in a constant surprise.

"What the hell do tree huggers know about bears and hunting?" Jack said. "They don't even come up here."

"They shut down the spring hunt?" Tom said, still surprised.

"Yea," said Jack. "Those wimps don't know nothin'. Why, hell, if they were here we'd hunt them."

We never doubted he meant what he said.

"Ever since they stopped the hunt, we've had bears coming into town, breaking into houses and camps, and they're scaring the hell out of the people.

"Seen any bears today?" Tom said.

"Not really," said Scott.

"What do you mean, 'not really'?"

"Well, we've been drinking since eight this morning and we thought we spotted a couple earlier, but hell, we don't know for sure and you don't want to shoot something if you're not sure what it is," said Scott shuffling his feet in the dirt.

Moonshadows

"Well, no," replied an amazed Tom.

"Now youse guys shouldn't think we're inebriated," said Jack. "We're fine. Why, hell, I say you're not drunk until you have to grab the grass to keep from falling off the edge of the earth."

"When you're grabbing grass, you're definitely drunk," Tom agreed.

We all laughed again, even though we had heard the line before.

"Where youse guys headed?" Jack asked.

"Nakina," I answered. "Then we board a float plane and fly north to fish the Albany River."

"Geez," said Jack. "The Albany is some wild country. Youse guys been there before?"

"Yes," said Tom. "This will be our fifth trip up to the Albany."

"Wow!" Scott said. "Youse guys are crazier than us."

"I don't think so," Sloan said.

We told a couple more stories, swatted mosquitoes together and finished our beer.

"Time to hit the road," Tom said.

"Terrific meeting up with youse guys," said Canada Jack.

"Me too," said Scott.

"Good luck bear hunting," said Charlie.

"Yea, you betcha," said Jack.

We got back in the van, now covered with a thick layer of dust.

Charlie started for the driver's door, but Tom stopped him.

"You're not driving while you're drinking," said Tom.

"Nobody is going anywhere until everyone finishes their beer and the empties are back in the case. If the provincial police catch us drinking and driving we'll spend our vacation in jail."

We slugged down the rest and got underway. I took the wheel.

The road started to become hilly, the roller coaster type.

"What have you been reading lately?" Tom asked Sloan.

"Deliverance, by James Dickey," said Sloan. "I'm almost done. Makes me think of us on some of our previous trips."

"As far as I recall no one on a past trip had to squeal like a pig," said Victor, "but I wonder how we would react in a similar situation."

17

Robert B. Gregg

Chapter 3

Deep in the forest I crested a small hill when Tom screamed, "Slow down!" His warning came too late. The car went airborne, barely clearing the hump at the top and, hitting the ground hard. We careened along the steep downward run.

I slammed on the brakes, but the momentum could not be overcome. The back of the van swung out to the side, and the whole vehicle spun out of control down the sharp slope.

At the bottom of the hill sat the railroad track that stripped the entire exhaust system off my car years before. We all prepared for the hit. A loud thud shook the vehicle.

Seatbelts slammed tight on our chests. Our gear went flying. The vehicle slid backwards into a brushy swamp. The accident happened and was over in a second.

We piled out through the mud and bushes, climbing over branches to survey the damage. "Not bad," said Charlie right away, without really looking at the situation. "We're alive."

"But can we push the van out of this muck," said Tom. "Mike, didn't you remember?"

"Sorry," I said, feeling stupid.

I got back in to drive as the others waded into the swamp to push. Victor, Tom and Sloan were pushing from the rear. Charlie was supervising.

"OK," said Tom. "Give her some gas."

I threw the shifter into low gear, but not gently enough, the wheels spun swamp and bog all over the pushers. They jumped back, but it was too late. They were covered in black gunk. Only their eyes and their mouths could be seen.

Despite laughing hysterically I kept the momentum going. The van struggled forward until it was back on the road.

"Everything seems OK, except us," said Sloan looking over the vehicle and laughing. "Thank God there's a stream here where we can wash up."

"Take it easy from now on," Tom said. "By the way, do you have any soap handy?" I pulled some shampoo and a towel from my backpack, wrapped the shampoo in the towel and handed them both to him.

"This will have to do for now," I said.

He joined Victor and Sloan in the stream. They took their clothes off and stood naked, batting mosquitoes and black flies and washing their outfits and themselves.

They were about finished when a big logging truck came down the hill and narrowly missed our van. He tooted his horn as he went by. We didn't know if he honked because we were parked on the wrong side of the road or because he was laughing at the naked guys.

Charlie and I were watching the show and trying to keep from falling into more sidesplitting laughter.

When everyone was clean and dry, we arranged the gear and piled back into the van. I continued until the pavement appeared.

We headed North to Highway 11 and turned west to Geraldton, where we proceeded North again to our destination. At the end of the farthest road north of Lake Superior was the town of Nakina, Ontario.

We saw numerous bears on the drive up, more than we had ever seen before. Canada Jack was right. The lack of a spring bear hunt boosted the bear population in Northern Ontario to a serious problem.

Six miles North of Geraldton, Sloan yelled, "Look at the size of that sow," pointing at a big female black bear eating grass alongside the road. She must have weighed close to 400 pounds.

We stopped to take some pictures and out of the heavy brush came two chubby cubs. As Tom rolled down the window to snap a photo, the mother bear decided she did not want snapshots taken of her babies and charged at the van.

We got out of there just in time as she swatted at the rear bumper. We looked back at the sow and her two cubs standing in the middle of the road, staring at us as we sped away.

"We don't need any more scratches on the car," said Charlie, concerned for the first time about the condition of Tom's vehicle.

"Thanks," said Tom sarcastically.

The Nakina road goes due North and is made up of gentle hills and broken pavement. The terrain varied from forest to cedar swamp. The big trees were gone now. A tangled jungle of pines, poplar and tamarack remained.

The sides of the road were mowed, and thick, bright green grasses lined the pavement. The springtime growth attracted the animals, mainly rabbits and bears, a strange combination.

Rock outcroppings mark the tops of many of the hills. Several of them topped off with an "Inuksuk," a pile of stones arranged to look like a human being. Inuksuk's are common along the roads of Northern Canada.

According to the Inuit, the first people to inhabit Arctic Canada, the Inuksuk acts in the capacity of a human being. In the far North, the Inuit place thousands of these figures across the landscape. Some are employed as hunting and navigation aids, while others have spiritual meanings.

Just south of Nakina the road comes to a Y. To the left is the road to Aroland, an Indian reserve and former German prisoner of war camp during World War II. Many of the outfitters who fly people North are located near Aroland. We would take the Aroland road in the morning.

We turned right to Nakina where we would spend the night. Nakina is the launching pad for hundreds of annual expeditions into Canada's Northern wilderness. The outfitters lure anglers, hunters and adventurers from all over the world to what the natives call "the bush."

The small town is centered on the old Canadian National depot, now turned into a boarding house and layover for those flying out the next day.

Numerous people talk and dream of coming here and going into the wilderness. Most never do.

The natives who live here lead a rough existence, but seem to prefer Nakina.

Many who grow up here go to cities like Winnipeg and Toronto to find work, but most return and are welcomed back with open arms. Every summer, the citizens of Nakina hold a "Welcome Back Reunion" for former residents and anyone else who cares to join in the celebration. Year after year, many return home. Some never leave again.

"The gathering offers those who have left a chance to correct their mistake," our guide Winston Wallace once told me. "We are a forgiving people."

The lakes North of Nakina were cut out of granite by huge glaciers. As the rivers of ice receded they left natural carvings. Many are touched by nature, including rock outcroppings painted with red, green, yellow and orange lichen.

Fast rivers, with rapids of whitewater, fill the lakes and then leave to fill others along their course. The lakes, in turn, feed and nourish the wildlife. They are filled with rocks from the glaciers and trees from the beaver.

The roar of floatplanes is a steady sound in the summer. The expeditions start near the end of May, after the spring thaw, and continue through the fall hunting season. Thousands of outdoorsmen are carried into the bush seeking adventure and escape from their "civilized" lives. They fly to pristine lakes and rivers surrounded by boreal forests. Some go on to the muskeg, tundra and barren lands.

When your adventure is finished you know yourself better and love those around you more. Life, your friends, and family become more important. A trip to the wilderness leaves you more appreciative of everything you have and kills the urge to simply want more. The further North you go the more you escape.

I always thought going on a trip like this was a true study in contrasts. The journey starts in the hustle and bustle of civilization and ends in the wild, and transports your soul from rat race to solitude. Going North is a way to find peace.

Every trip North changed me. Each of us was affected in our own way. As we grew older, we came to realize the true value of every trip. Each trip became more precious, because every adventure put us closer to the final one.

Chapter 4

We came around a curve and spotted a sign on the shoulder of the road, 'Nakina. Population 500.' At last, we had arrived. The sign was always a welcome sight that the long drive was over. As we drove through the town it seemed abandoned, but then Nakina always seemed abandoned.

We zigzagged down a couple of side streets and headed for the old railroad depot, now a boarding house, where we would spend the night.

The depot had been recently renovated because the town needed rooms to accommodate the construction crews that would build the new paper mill.

We pulled into the parking lot as the sun began to set. We parked next to the Laundromat. A young Indian woman with two children entered to do their wash.

Tom and I went to check in. Sloan and Victor proceeded around to the back to take their annual hike down the railroad tracks. Charlie tagged along with them.

As Tom and I entered the office, the man at the counter said, "Hello, can I help you?"

"Name's Sullivan. I made reservations for five tired fishermen who need rooms for the night," Tom said.

"Yep, your rooms are ready. The price is thirty dollars per man, and you each get your own room."

"That's fine," said Tom.

"Take 101, 102, 103, 104 and 106," the man said. "There's a towel on each bed and the showers are at the end of the hall."

"What happened to room 105?" I asked.

"Not renovated yet."

"We're going to get something to eat first and maybe hit the tavern for a couple of beers," Tom said. "Do we need a key to get in the main door?"

"Usually," the man said, "but I'll be around to let you in. I also run the restaurant. See you soon."

Robert B. Gregg

Chapter 5

The railroad yard at Nakina never changed. The same old ties and steel wheels still lay rusting on the ground behind the depot. Looking from the old building, the perspective of the tracks going west is amazing. The tracks run straight and true to somewhere far out on the horizon.

They go on from here to towns like Winnipeg, Regina, Moose Jaw, Medicine Hat, Calgary and others, past the wheat fields of the Canadian prairies, and through the majestic Rocky Mountains.

The setting sun greeted Sloan and Victor as they took their annual walk down the tracks. The warm weather was unusual for early June in Nakina. The mosquitoes and black flies swarmed around them and attacked their ears and nose. They didn't go far before the bugs drove them back.

"I'm getting eaten alive," Victor shouted. "Let's get the hell out of here." They quickly agreed and returned to us on the run. As they came rushing around the building, Tom and I emerged from the boarding house.

"You fellows in a hurry?" Tom asked them.

"The bugs are horrible on the other side of the depot," said Victor. "They're not so bad over here. More wind."

"I think I need a transfusion," said Sloan. "I lost a lot of blood."

"We're all set," said Tom. "We each have our own room. A towel is on the bed and the shower is at the end of the hall."

"Do you have the keys?" Charlie asked.

"Keys?" said Tom. "This is Nakina. We don't need any stinking keys. Anybody hungry?"

"Yea," I answered.

"Yes. Starved," said Sloan.

"OK then," said Tom.

"The restaurant is right here," he said, pointing to a door about 60 feet away.

We ordered burgers and fries, ate quickly and made for the saloon about a block away to drink beer and take in a hockey game.

"I hope they have satellite TV so we can watch the Stanley Cup playoffs," said Charlie as we walked down the street. "The Avalanche should be playing the Red Wings tonight."

Although born and raised in the Denver area, Charlie became an avid

Detroit Red Wing fan after moving to Michigan. The toughest thing about going North, Charlie told us, was missing the playoffs.

The wind picked up even more and the mosquitoes disappeared. A bizarre purple and orange sky made for a gorgeous evening. As we approached the bar, a big homemade sign hanging above the door caught our eyes.

'Tonight Only, Straight from Thunder Bay. EXOTIC DANCERS.'

"Is this for real?" Charlie said. "Exotic dancers in Nakina?"

We entered and took a table in front of the TV.

The early game between the Montreal Canadians and the San Jose Sharks had already started. About thirty people drank beer and intently watched every play.

Over our shoulders, we observed an overweight, naked woman dancing on the stage in the adjoining room. She didn't strike me as exotic. Four very inebriated men stared at her.

We sat at the table having beers, watching the game, and talking about how great the fishing would be. We told stories to one another about previous trips. We all heard them before. We politely listened anyway.

Charlie decided to interrupt the conversation with a joke.

"Did you hear about the big Naval conference?" Charlie said

"No," I answered.

"Well, just last week a U.S. Navy Admiral attended a conference that included admirals from the U.S., British, Canadian, Australian and French Navies. At a cocktail party reception, he was standing with a group of half dozen or so officers.

"Everyone chatted away in English as they sipped their drinks, but a French admiral complained that, whereas Europeans learn many languages, Americans speak only English.

He asked, 'Why is it that we always have to speak English in these conferences rather than French?' Without hesitating, a British Admiral replied, "Maybe because we Brits, Canadians, Aussies and Americans arranged it so you wouldn't have to speak German."

We all roared. Even the Indians at the next table got a kick out of the story.

Native Americans made up a majority of the population in the bar and in town. The older men are weather-beaten from their lives outdoors.

Many worked as trappers and guides. Some were employed as lumberjacks for Kimberly-Clark, one of the area's largest employers.

We listened as Tom explained, in detail, what would happen over the next week and why he didn't want anyone taking foolish chances. He said all this to people who had been there before, and our novice, Charlie.

"The Albany is a dangerous river," he said leaning his elbows on the small table. "Most of it is fast and the rest of it is faster. There are waterfalls, cataracts and rapids, lots of waterfalls, cataracts and rapids."

"The last time we went to the Albany we almost lost Tom," Sloan interjected. "His canoe hit a huge rock in the middle of the rapids and disappeared. We found him downstream clinging to a log. We rescued him or he would have drowned."

A look of embarrassment appeared on Tom's face. "I was fine," Tom said slowly shaking his head.

"What time do we fly out in the morning?" Charlie asked Tom.

"We're on the first plane north. We have to be on the dock at six," said Tom. "We better get over to the hotel and hit the sack."

"What about the Red Wing game?" said Charlie.

"They're playing the Avalanche. The game is in Denver, and doesn't start until 10 PM. that's way too late for us," said Tom.

We quickly finished our beers.

Night came swiftly, and the temperature was near freezing. We shivered on the walk back. .

Every room at the boarding house had either two twin beds or a bunk bed. The renovated depot was not very busy, that's probably why we each got our own room. Sleep came quickly after a long day on the road.

Before we knew it, Tom knocked on our doors with instructions

"Rise and shine! Get your butts moving. It's 5 am and we've got a 10 mile drive on logging roads just to get to the plane!"

We got up, showered, dressed and met at the van.

The sun had begun to rise and the air was bitter cold, but then the mornings are always cold in Nakina in early June. Standing in the dirt parking lot, we could see our breath as we waited for Tom to pay the bill.

"We're about to leave civilization, men," Victor said to the shivering group as Tom approached the vehicle.

"Time to head to the Great White North," Tom added.

We jumped in the van, excited as little kids.

After a brief, but bumpy ride, we were the first group to arrive at the outfitters building, which stood on the top of a small hill overlooking a lake. The building was near the dock where the plane that would take us North was tied.

We walked into the building.

"Welcome back men," said Evelyn, a good-natured woman who ran the accounting part of business. "Good to see you fellas again."

"Good to be back, Evelyn," said Tom.

"You betcha," she said. "The alternative wouldn't be good for you or us. After all, you fellas are getting older."

We smiled, stared at the pictures of lucky anglers, and checked out the mounted fish on the walls, and drank coffee, and took turns going to the bathroom.

We all paid our share of the remaining outfitter's fee in cash, asked about the fishing, and went down to the dock for the "weigh-in."

We placed every item on the huge scale. We were allowed 100 pounds per man, not including ourselves. To make sure the plane wasn't overloaded, we were also weighed. Flying north is serious business. An overloaded bush plane could prove an unforgiving mistake.

The head of the dock crew gassed up the plane, OK'd us for take off, and gave us a slip of paper for the pilot. Tom tipped the crew, who helped us carry our supplies, and they left us alone and went up the gravel hill back to the building for coffee.

Chapter 6

We stood on a concrete dock looking toward the North, waiting for our pilot.

The lake seemed eerily quiet; the water was still.

A gentle breeze softly moved the rushes on the shore, clearing the morning mist. The glow of the sun was just barely showing in the distance

Several small birds broke the silence, their wings beating against the air as they dove for insects and moved quickly down the edge of the water.

Tall spruce, tamarack, birches, cedar and white pine gazed majestically at the lake as they had for countless years. Truly a place of beauty and peace.

A bright orange DeHavilland Otter with pontoons rested in the water next to the dock. Our shadows cast long by the rising sun.

Tom smiled. We all smiled.

"This is going to be quite a trip," he said.

"You bet," exclaimed Victor, usually reserved and controlled.

"No kidding," said Charlie, eager as a ten-year-old.

Sloan grinned a contented grin. Sloan gave the impression he was born a fisherman. Since he was old enough to walk he had fished. As he got older, his father took him hunting for black bear and whitetail deer, but fishing remained his favorite love.

In the fall he would catch Chinook and Coho salmon in streams running into Lake Michigan. During the summer, he made weekend trips to Michigan's Upper Peninsula to fish for trout with his dad.

Sloan told us he stopped hunting about ten years ago, because the fall trout fishing had become better than the hunting.

As a teenager his father started taking him on annual fly-in trips into the Canadian wilderness North of Lake Superior. He loved the wilderness. If he knew one thing for sure, he knew he belonged here, his favorite place.

He was named Sloan after his father's brother who died fighting a forest fire. His uncle was a real hero. "A heroic man, who gave up his life for his men," Sloan once told us.

According to Sloan, his father cried whenever he talked about his brother and how he saved his men. It was the only time he saw his father cry.

We stood with Sloan by the lake now, waiting.

The pilot was due soon, and he would take us up over the endless trees, into the bush; into the land we knew well, the true wilderness the tourists never see.

Summer after summer we returned. This trip, however, would be a special one. We were going back to Grassi Lake, a widening of the massive Albany River. This wasn't just a fishing trip for the monster brook trout, walleyes and pike.

This expedition was for memories and friendship.

We stacked our gear on the dock like cordwood. We had duffels containing our clothes and the equipment we would need, and tubes with our fishing rods safely inside. Everything was piled up, ready to go, along with sleeping bags and two huge coolers packed with food.

And there were six cases of beer.

We took a case for each of us, and two for Charlie. We knew there would be nothing left when the trip ended.

As the sun slowly rose in the sky the morning chill left our bodies. We all felt the excitement. It was the beginning of what would be a great adventure.

"God, this is a wonderful day," Tom said.

"You bet your life," said Sloan, repeating his favorite saying.

"I'll go along with that," said Victor, who usually went along with everything. We all smiled. We felt great. We gazed out over the lake again admiring the sunrise.

Suddenly the quiet of dawn was broken. The rumbling sound of a car bouncing down a gravel road became louder and louder. We could see it now. A cloud of dust came at the dock with an old Jeep inside it.

The Jeep skidded to a stop a few feet from the lake. The door opened and a man sprung out. He possessed an extraordinary face fashioned by the outdoors, and his bright and cheerful eyes beamed from under a bushy, black beard tinged with gray.

The man's jacket an old anorak, the kind the Indians and Inuit wear, but not made of sealskins. His was made of nylon. It bore a hood, now plastered down on his back, and a pull-tie snugged it around his waist, a useful thing for the varying weather of the North.

His old, worn wool shirt might have been a good one, like an L.L. Bean. His well-worn jeans covered with stains that ran the gamut from engine oil to what looked like mustard.

"You rascals. Welcome home," he said with an ever-present smile.

"It's good to be back, Ray," Tom replied happily as they hugged and shook hands.

"We've missed you Ray, you old bugger," I said. Ray wanted no more hugs. He walked toward the dock.

"A good day to fly," Ray said looking into the sky. "Let's load this baby and get the hell out of here."

Ray seemed around 80, although we found out Ray celebrated his 56th birthday the previous July.

Living outdoors in the sun and wind took its toll on his face, but he had the athletic body of a young man.

A bush pilot since age 16, Ray remained an independent man. He had never married, a fact that didn't surprise us.

Now he stared off into the sky, a bright blue from horizon to horizon. The trees made a perfect reflection in the glassy water.

He glanced at Tom. "Well you better start tellin' me what you've been up to before we get into the air. You know I can't hear a thing after the engine starts."

Before Tom answered, Ray spoke again. "How's your mom?"

"She's doing well. She doesn't know who she is, but she's strong as hell and healthy," said Tom. "The doctors think she's got Alzheimer's."

"I hope she gets better," said Ray.

Tom began to tell Ray how Alzheimer's patients don't get better, but decided to let the conversation drop.

Ray walked back to the jeep to get a small cooler containing his lunch. He loaded it with a Pepsi and a ginger ale he took from a larger cooler. He never drank booze when he flew, but he could really put it away when he wasn't.

We started loading. Beer and the two big coolers went on first, followed by gear and food boxes, rod cases, then things like waders, with landing nets and backpacks thrown on top.

"Hey Tom! Get your ass over here and help us load," said Charlie.

"I'm getting too old for this. I've got to save my strength for drinking beer and battling fish."

"You couldn't catch a fish if you were an eagle," Tom answered.

Charlie's eyes brightened. He was amused by the comment.

Ray walked back to the plane with Tom, "You got enough food in this thing for ten men," Ray said as they loaded one of the big coolers.

"How is Winston?" Tom asked.

"Winston is the same as ever," said Ray. "He's a piece of work. We already flew him in; he's waiting for you."

Winston Wallace guided us, off and on, for years. Fact is, Winston, Tom and I once appeared on the cover of Field & Stream. Tom played the "lucky angler" in the front of the canoe. I'm the guy hoisting the monster pike out of the water in a huge landing net. Winston sat in the stern with a paddle in his hand.

The photo is a classic, showing us with surprised looks on our faces. Truth be told, the fish had been dead for two days and jerking the monster up hard and fast became the only way we could make it look alive. The picture came out great and we never miss a chance to tell everyone we once graced the cover of Field & Stream, the January 1978 issue.

I still have that cover in a glass frame back home in Oxford. I'm proud of it.

We always went north at about the same time every year. Just after the big spring "breakup," when the river's rising water pushes up the ice from below, creating huge jams that eventually explode with tremendous force.

The breakup is the major reason for change in the directions of rivers of the North.

The Albany River is an ever-changing body of water where Winston guided bear hunters in the spring before what he called "the tree huggers in Toronto" put an end to the spring hunt. To make a living, he guides fishermen in the summer and moose hunters in the fall.

Winter, however, was his favorite time of the year. He ran trap lines, in the snow, along the same rivers he guided in the summer. He trapped wolf, beaver, fox, lynx and anything else he could catch, sell, mount or make into rugs.

We had finished packing the plane when Tom asked Ray to check the

Moonshadows

load. Ray went inside the fuselage, tied a net down over the boxes and gear, gave Tom the thumbs up, turned and shouted at us. "Get your asses on board! I haven't got all day." Victor, Charlie, Sloan and Tom got in, anxious to get going.

Ray stepped onto the pontoon, jumping into the high pilot seat with the zeal of a kid of 18. I followed, going in the side door, and then moving up between the others to the "co-pilot" seat.

Ray pushed the knobs, spun the little wheels, and pulled the levers, and The DeHavilland Otter started to roar.

The choice of many bush pilots, the Otter is a workhorse of an airplane, reliable, strong, and carries a full load. The only problem is the noise. The Otter is one of the loudest planes ever made, with its smaller cousin, The Beaver, a close second.

The morning mist slowly lifted off the lake. Ray cranked the engine up even more, and soon the Otter roared louder. We were ready to go.

"Tighten your seat belts!" Ray yelled. "We are off, gentlemen. I've got places to go and people to see, and you've got fish to catch."

He throttled the engine up again, testing its response. The prop whipped the wind, and we motored away from the dock heading for the far end of the lake at a fast clip.

We taxied down to the far end of the lake, and Ray turned the plane around in a small cove still partially frozen with shoreline ice, and aimed us straight across the water at a stand of high trees.

He opened the throttle, and we were soon barreling down the water. The tall dark forest stood like a barricade in a crescent bay at the end of the lake.

Ray spun wheels, cranked knobs, pulled levers and glanced at the gauges as we neared the dark, green wall approaching faster as we sped toward it, in what is always an anxious moment. No matter how often you took off, you were never quite sure you would make it.

Suddenly, as the forest seemed to black out the sky, the plane lifted and the wings cleared the tops of the trees. We are airborne.

Ray turned and smiled at us. He was in the sky and the sky was his home. "Sorry. No stewardesses," Ray yelled back over the noise. "No food. No coffee. No service of any kind. If you have to piss, use the coffee can under Tom's seat."

33

We laughed and stared out the small windows at the forest below. Looking down at the countless lakes, rivers, creeks, and beaver ponds was always a sobering experience.

The first thing we noticed was how far the clear-cut had expanded since the previous year. It always seemed too far. Every year, the forest would disappear in large bites. The government and the logging companies replanted trees every summer, but they never seemed to catch up with the logging.

Sloan pointed down and said to Charlie, "Some of these lakes and rivers still haven't been fished. Some day I'd like to say I fished them all."

"You're out of your mind," Charlie yelled back. "You look at anything with water and all you can think of is fishing. You're out of your mind."

We flew around a big storm, passed over a clear-cut and headed North towards the Opichuan River. We asked Ray to fly up the Opichuan to the Albany so we might bring back memories. He agreed.

"The Opichuan is one of my favorites, too," he told us before we left.

The Opichuan is not a large stream, but carries its tannin-colored waters swiftly through narrow lakes on its way to feed the Albany. Full of whitewater rapids and brook trout, we had fished the fast-flowing stream on previous trips.

"Let's take a closer look!" Ray yelled over the roar of the engine. We dropped down and followed the river. We surveyed the wilderness below. Ray pointed forward and said, "There she is."

On the far horizon a mighty river presented itself, and the huge watershed it formed. High from snowmelt and spring rains, a massive river meandered into several side channels, but the main stream was easy to distinguish. The Albany lay straight ahead.

The river starts up in Northern Manitoba and passes through a region of rugged, Precambrian bedrock. The river has spent thousands of years cutting its way through granite, mud and clay on the way to Hudson Bay and the ocean.

And now, we had arrived at our destination. Grassi Lake was formed between two sets of the Albany's rapids. We had started our descent when Victor noticed another plane at the cabin across from ours.

Moonshadows

"We've got neighbors," he said. A dark green floatplane was tied to their dock.

We glided to a soft landing. You could hear the water spraying under the pontoons as the plane touched down and aimed toward our rustic cabin on the shore. We drifted slowly, engine running, toward the floating dock in front of the cabin.

It was still early morning and we could see the smoke of a fire rising from its chimney. The cabin was nestled into the woods.

Nearing the shore, Ray cut the throttle and the plane coasted to a gentle bump alongside the dock. "We have arrived, gentlemen," said Tom, who quickly got up, opened the side door and climbed down the plane's small ladder.

Our guide, Winston "Grey Wolf" Wallace, stood between the dock and the cabin, and keenly observed us as we arrived.

"What is he thinking?" I wondered as I disembarked. I always believed Winston lived constantly in deep thought.

The morning dew still covered the grass. A faint breeze blew in the direction of the river's current from west to east.

The cabin stood no different than three years before, our last trip here. The lake seemed bigger, the high springtime floodwater spreading its width and breadth.

"Welcome to Grassi Lake and the great Albany River," Winston said as he came down to the dock. "It's nice to see you fellows once more."

"It's good to be back," said Victor with a grin.

Winston stepped toward the plane and, without a word we formed a line and, with Ray's help, started unloading the cargo. The gear came off in the reverse order and soon we were finished.

Tom gave Ray a $50 bill.

"That's way too much," Ray said, trying to hand back the money.

"It's not enough," said Tom. "You got us here safely, and you can't put a price on that."

"That's my job," said Ray.

"Keep it, and don't argue with the customer."

Ray smiled, put the money in his jacket pocket, climbed back into the pilot's seat, and started the engine. The Otter roared ready to go. He slid his window open, and yelled to us over the noise.

"I'll do a check flight on Sunday around noon. I'll be back to pick you up Thursday. Meanwhile, like I said, I've got places to go and people to see."

The plane slowly moved offshore to the middle of the lake and taxied downstream with the current, stopped, turned, and sped straight back across the water, taking flight right in front of us.

We shaded our eyes and watched the plane leave the same way it came, disappearing over the trees, heading south for the base camp.

We were alone. The wilderness became ours for the taking.

"You're in my hands now," Winston said cheerfully.

Grey Wolf possessed a weathered face partially hidden by pitch-black hair. He was rough and strong for his size and could out run and out muscle any man I know. His wife was back in Geraldton and four grown sons were scattered across Canada.

A family man and a church-going Catholic, Winston loved the "bush" as he called it. On all but the worst of nights he would take his sleeping bag outside and slumber on the ground.

"I prefer being outside," he once told me. "Under the moon and the stars is where God intended man to sleep." He usually complied with this philosophy, but if it rained or snowed he moved inside, snug under a roof with us.

I challenged him once on his wavering philosophy about not sleeping outdoors in bad weather, and he replied: "Do I look like a fool?" I did not answer.

Our cabin was nestled in the woods just past a clearing, where beavers had dropped some freshly cut poplar and birch near the dock, very close to the boats.

We formed a line from the dock to the cabin and handed gear and boxes forward with vigor. Winston handed to Charlie, then Victor, Tom, Sloan and finally to me, the person who rushed in and out.

A square building 24 feet wide by 24 feet long, the cabin faced southeast to catch the morning sun. It was of simple construction, made of three basic materials, four by eight foot pieces of plywood, two by four's and nails.

Inside, were three sets of bunk beds on one wall opposite a propane stove and refrigerator, which sat at each end of a sink and counter top. The wood stove, made from a 55-gallon oil drum, was located near the entrance.

A picnic table sat square in the middle. There were six chairs at the table, and two wooden folding chairs against the back wall. There were cupboards above the counter and shelves near the large rear window. Two Coleman lanterns hung on hooks screwed into an overhead cross beam.

The bunks were perfect for the six of us. Each man's bunk was made up of 2 by 4's with a 4' by 8' sheet of plywood for a bed. On top of the plywood was an eggshell foam mattress. We laid our sleeping bags on top of the mattress, and after each day of adventure, we crawled in and slept like we were at the Ritz-Carlton.

Each of us kept a flashlight or headlamp by our bunk for emergencies or simply midnight treks to use the outhouse. Our duffels sat under the lower bunk and could be conveniently pulled out to get whatever we needed.

The fishing gear was kept outside near the boats so it didn't have to be carried back and forth every day. We brought the life jackets in every night so they would stay dry.

When we finished stocking the shelves and cupboards with groceries, and filling the refrigerator, we looked at one another and smiled.

We were back home.

Time to go fishing.

Robert B. Gregg

Chapter 7

Sloan and Tom and I decided to take the long run to the west end of the lake and fish the Albany. The river entered the lake around a narrow island, dividing into two sets of whitewater rapids. The three of us had fished the rapids before and caught some beautiful brook trout. Expectations ran high.

Victor, Winston and Charlie decided to catch some walleyes for dinner, along the other shore, opposite our cabin. We were surprised Victor didn't go with us, because Tom told me he had lost a monster trout in these rapids three years previous and never stopped talking about getting revenge.

The morning sun gave a glow to Tom's grinning face as he ran the 9.9 horsepower engine at full throttle. I sat facing Sloan and Tom. We seemed to be flying. A huge wake chased the boat. The trees along the nearby shore zoomed by.

Approaching whitewater, we motored right up to the middle island and started fishing from the boat. We caught nothing and after about an hour we decided to try the rapids just upstream.

After crossing the swift current, we jumped out and pulled the boat safely onto the gravel beach below the rapids. We put our waders on. A narrow portage trail led us along the bank. Everything was still wet from the morning rain, and the soft muskeg was laden with animal tracks. The path seemed to be more a moose path than a portage.

A deep pool waited at the end of the trail, my favorite from previous years. Tom started casting at the top of the rapids where he also had lost a big fish last year. I moved upstream about 200 feet. Sloan started casting halfway between us.

I used a nice Sage fly rod with 6-pound test leader and a two-inch stonefly. I drifted the fly with the current.

The rapids stretched out ahead of us as far as the eye could see. The river ran through a cathedral of springtime green forest. The Albany flew by us; the volume of water was astounding. A light morning fog still floated over the back bays and eddies where the sun had yet to touch.

"Work fast," I thought. "Work fast and find the big ones." I am a speed fisherman. My theory is the more water you cover and the more casts you make, the more fish you catch.

Robert B. Gregg

If fish are hungry, they'll hit right away. I don't believe in spending a whole lot of time trying to convince an uncooperative fish to strike. I'm on to the cooperative fish.

Tom, on the other hand, is methodical and persistent. If he believes a good size trout is in a hole or run, he will fish the spot to death with every fly at his disposal before he gives up and moves on.

After years of using my method, and Tom his, I have decided through a personal, non-scientific, survey that both work.

Sloan didn't budge from his spot.

I spent an unusual amount of time, 30 minutes, at the pool. I caught three respectable whitefish around four pounds each, but no trout. I had several other whitefish on, but lost them when the hook pulled out of their soft mouths.

Using a spare stringer, I tied the whitefish to the branch of a dead tree lying in the shallows and left them swimming on the edge of the pool. We would, at least, have whitefish for dinner, and they are delicious poached.

"Keep an eye on these," I yelled to Sloan. He nodded in the affirmative. I headed further upstream. "You never know when a hungry mink or otter will attempt to steal your fish," I yelled back to him.

The next set of rapids was treacherous. I hugged the shore to avoid being knocked on my ass, as rushing water pulled at my legs, and the gravel bottom seemed like ball bearings under my feet. You needed a good sense of balance to keep from going over your waders and getting soaked.

I found a shallow back-eddy to stand in and cast a big fly across a narrow, deep pool; the fly soon caught in the current rushing by a big rock. I furiously stripped the line, trying to keep up with the flow of the water.

The effort seemed worthless. If you don't keep the fly moving at the speed of the current, the fish usually won't hit because the bait doesn't look natural?

Then the line switched directions from downstream to upstream. At first I thought I had hung up on the rock, but the line quickly went taut, zinging and zipping through the river. My rod bent over and throbbed. I spotted him in the clear water. This is what I came for, a big brook trout of enormous size.

He shot back towards me across the narrow pool so fast the line went slack and I thought I lost him. I reeled faster and pulled back on the rod. The fish was still there, pulsating in the current. I could see him about 30 feet away thrashing his head from side to side. The fish splashed and twisted, its brilliant colors flashing in the rays of the sun.

I waded toward the shore, not wanting to push my light line to it's limit, but I knew that the more time the fish fought the less of a chance I had of landing him.

He hung in the fast current, playing hard to get. He wouldn't budge. After a short upstream run, he slipped behind a series of rocks and tried to rest. Time to put the pressure on him. If you let any fish rest long enough you have to fight it all over again.

Lifting my rod high, I tried to use leverage to move the fish out from behind the rocks, but he wouldn't come.

I took another step back towards shore and lifted as high as I could. The extra leverage did the trick. The trout slid out from the boulders and I skimmed the fish across the surface on its side into my net, not giving it a chance to swim.

It was a beautiful specimen of speckled trout about 21 inches long. A creamy white trim on the fins accentuated the dark greenish back, which blended into a brilliant orange belly. Small dark red dots, each circled in a faint halo of blue, were scattered randomly on the top half of the body. A vermicular design covered its back.

The trout retained a slightly hooked jaw, the sign of a male, and I found out later that black stonefly nymphs filled its stomach. I tied the fish to a fallen tree with a piece of heavy fishing line. I'd pick it up later. I marked the tree with my blue Buff sun scarf.

Nothing could go wrong after such a wonderful start to the day.

We only keep one trout apiece per day for dinner. We returned the rest to the river.

Wading through two more sets of rapids, I came to a place where the river widened over a shallow bar. The gravel at my feet fascinated me. The stones mainly polished dark granite, were probably ore bearing.

Constantly polished and shined by the fine black and beige sand that was moved along by the river for thousands of years. The sunlight glistened off the beautiful stones.

The waters of the Albany shimmered in the morning glow just before dropping swiftly through a hundred yards of rapids. "What a day!" I said out loud, and looked around to see if anyone caught me talking to myself.

The gravel bar extended all the way across the river and below it was a shaded area at the head of the pool on the other side. I thought the spot might be the hideout of a big fish.

Double hauling my fly line, I arched a long cast into the dark waters, and readied myself for the strike. Two strips of the line and I felt a hard pull. My rod pumped again, but this time, the fish bent it double.

My reel let line out at a furious pace. My drag was set properly, not too tight, not too loose, but this trout was powerful. You could hear the line cut the water as the fish rushed full-speed upstream.

I thought of tightening my drag, but that's almost always a bad thing when playing a fish.

Cranking whenever I could get line, I arched my rod to the side and waded up the river after the runaway trout. The fish zigged and zagged through the rapids, swimming fast toward a huge, dead tree lying broadside in the shallows.

I applied more pressure. The fish needed to be stopped or I would lose him in that dead tree

The fish jumped, slamming itself into the tree's limbs, half in and half out of the water and back down into the river again. The line went slack. I reeled fast in the desperate hope that the trout had turned and swam toward me. The line stayed slack.

The fish was gone forever, but he will always be in my memories.

I caught just a brief glimpse of the trout, but how big it may have been, I could only guess. My imagination went wild. I couldn't turn the monster around. The trout possessed the power of a sizable salmon.

I checked my drag. It worked fine. At the end of the line, the leader was frayed. The trout probably rubbed the line on the log.

Wading to shore, I sat down on a rock. Adrenaline still pumped through my veins. I trembled from the exciting duel in the sun. I lost, but the loss really didn't matter. It had been an honorable fight with an honorable foe.

There was, as always, a feeling of disappointment in losing a monster. It would have been cool to have a better look at the fish, but somehow being able to imagine the size is even better.

I pulled a beer out of my backpack and drank away the thirst, watching the sun glisten on the rapids.

I waded back in and worked downstream. As I came around a bend I saw Tom sitting on a boulder on a narrow spit of island in the middle of the whitewater. He tied on a new fly and didn't notice me. Sloan lingered a hundred yards upstream in the shallows working his fly rod. I had passed him when I hiked the path and never noticed him.

Tom is a purist of sorts. It is beneath his dignity to catch a trout on anything but a dry fly.

As I got ready to call to Tom, a crunching and crashing noise came from the woods on my right. Just above me, upstream from Tom, came a newly born moose calf at full speed. Eyes bugged out and terrorized, the calf hit the rapids at full speed and tried to swim across the river. The gangly animal had trouble, and the current swept it down to Tom and the small island no more than 40 feet long.

Tom stood up and stepped aside as the calf tried to get its footing on the rocks.

Soon, another crashing sound came out of the woods and into the river. A gigantic mama moose with fury in her eyes launched her body into the rapids and appeared at Tom's feet in just seconds. She had no problem handling the fast water.

Tom moved to the head of the little island as the mother and her calf came ashore to share the other end that, just a few seconds before, was Tom's alone.

The mother moose glanced at Tom, stared at her calf, and jumped into the rapids. The calf followed. They swam together to the other side and disappeared into the forest, crashing through the woods as they left the river behind.

At that moment several wolves howled at the top of the ridge. We pretty much figured out what happened. The wolves probably tried to take the calf and the mother fought them off. More than likely, the calf left first and mom followed.

I called to Tom, "That was pretty exciting."

"I thought I was in a mess of trouble. I had nowhere to go and that mother was huge. Did you see the whole thing?"

"Yes," I said. "I wish I had my GoPro camera with me, but it's back at the cabin."

I waded over to the island and we each caught a couple of small trout.

Tom had fished there all morning and caught six trout. The biggest one he kept on his stringer. The fish weighed close to four pounds.

Sloan, who was fishing the rapids above us and never heard a thing, soon waded down to join us.

"Tough fishing," he said. Tom and I looked at him in surprise.

"Yea. I guess," said Tom, looking at me and winking. We sat down on the shore and drank a beer together.

"I was thinking," Sloan said to us.

"Not again," I interrupted laughing. "You did this once before, about three years ago."

"No, really," Sloan said with a serious look on his face.

Sloan contemplated the brilliant, sunlit woods on the other side of the river. "You know a trip up here has many compensations. There is no real sense of property," he said. "No fences. No houses."

He stood and held his arms straight out from his sides. "What you see, no matter how far or how wonderful, is yours. Your personal estate."

He turned in a circle with his arms still out. "Your rivers, your lakes, your trees, your hills," he continued. "And no matter how rich someone is, they can't buy it. They can't take it away from you. That's what's great about coming up here."

Chapter 8

Winston motored the boat across the massive river. The current was as strong as he had seen in the Albany.

"No problem. Get ready," he reassured Charlie and Victor, who went about rigging their lines with yellow jigs they hoped would catch walleye for dinner.

Once past the main flow, they sped up and were headed to one of Winston's favorite walleye holes, downstream from the long grassy island situated directly across from our cabin. As they rounded the bend to work their way along the shore, they spotted three men in a boat trolling at high speed in a nearby cove.

"Must be the guys from the other cabin," said Victor. "But what the hell are they doing? They're going way too fast to catch fish."

They shook their heads in disbelief and motored on to the hole Winston thought would produce some walleye. They anchored and started jigging.

Victor caught a small Northern and released it. Charlie jigged until his arm was about to fall off, then quit fishing altogether. "I'm going to relax for awhile," said Charlie, "Let you catch dinner."

"OK. That's enough talk," interrupted Winston. "Let's start catching fish. Time to change baits gentlemen."

He instructed them to put on a four-inch Daredevle Five-of-Diamond spoon. The lure was an elongated spoon-shaped piece of thick metal, painted a golden yellow color and was decorated with five spaced out, red diamond-shaped figures. The spoon didn't look like anything fish feed on, but many of the best fishing lures don't.

"Let them flutter to the bottom and jig 'em up like you do the jigs," Winston said. "We've got to wake these fish up."

Charlie dropped his straight down over the side of the boat and pulled up. Bang! "Fish on!" Charlie bellowed.

They caught a dozen walleye in fifteen minutes. They kept six eating size ones for dinner. Then, as fast as the action started, they stopped hitting.

"We've got dinner," said Victor. "Now let's go after a monster."

"I've got the spot," said Grey Wolf as he cranked up the motor. "Take in the anchor."

Winston guided them through the heavy current above the downstream rapids. The whitewater was full of huge boulders and surged around each one creating individual whirlpools behind them.

"Cast some #5 Mepps spinners with bucktails," said Winston. "Reel them in slowly, just under the surface, and let the current pull them around the rocks."

Victor pitched his lure near the bank and was retrieving when a huge wake came off the shore and headed towards his bait.

"Get ready," Winston yelled. "Let him take it."

Victor excitedly turned the crank, barely able to control himself. Ten feet from the boat, the surface of the water exploded. A monster Northern pike hammered his lure and was now swimming away. The fish headed downstream with the current, thrashing hard with its tail.

"Holy Shit!" Charlie yelled. "Hang on Victor!"

Winston followed the fish with the boat until they got dangerously close to the falls. "This is as far as we go," Winston said. "You'll have to bring him to us."

Victor's drag was as tight as possible. Still, you could hear the reel letting out line. He couldn't turn the monster.

"I'm going to lose him," Victor said in a desperate voice.

"No you're not. Use your leverage," Winston said. "Make him work."

Victor lifted hard on his rod and it doubled over.

"OK now. Bring your pole to the side," said Winston. "Keep up the leverage and you can direct the fish better. Push the butt of your rod towards him. Use the bend for even more power."

Victor made the rod work the fish. His face was red, but happy and determined. He picked up some line.

"You got him coming," said Winston. "Keep the pressure on him."

The battle went on for several minutes. The fish began to tire.

"I'll get the net," said Charlie.

"No," admonished Winston. "This fish will not fit in any net we have on board.

"When you get him close Victor, move him over to me. Steady now."

The huge pike was coming to the boat now. Victor could feel it weaken.

"Keep him coming to me," advised Winston when he saw Victor rest.

Moonshadows

Victor heaved up on his pole and the pike came to the top. The fish was wallowing. Victor was winning the battle.

"Move him around to my side," Winston said, still holding the boat steady above the rapids.

Victor stood and slid the monster toward the guide.

Holding the motor handle in one hand for balance, Winston reached down into the water with the other and slid it along the pike's back, and grabbed the Northern behind the gills and lifted the fish straight up out of the water.

"Now that's huge," he said proudly, holding the thrashing fish in one hand, while motoring back upstream.

Victor's face was one big smile. Charlie was like a little kid. "That's the biggest pike I've ever seen," Charlie said. "Must weigh 35 pounds. What do you think, Winston?"

"Well, this Northern's a beauty all right, but closer to 23 or 24 pounds."

They sped to the calm, shallow water to take some pictures. Arriving in a small cove, Winston put the fish on its own metal stringer, using two loops instead of the usual one. The big pike dwarfed the walleyes on the other stringer. He attached the pike stringer to the oarlock.

"We don't want him to get away now do we?" Winston told them.

Victor took the camera out of his backpack and handed it to Grey Wolf. "Would you take some pictures?" Victor pleaded.

"Sure," said Winston. "Hold him up."

Victor unhooked the stringer from the oarlock and reached into the water. With a good grip he lifted the pike up, straining to hold him out front, making the fish look even bigger.

Charlie was awestruck at the size of the fish.

Winston took a couple of pictures vertically and then asked Victor if he wanted to hold the pike horizontally for another shot.

"That would be great," said Victor. He put the fish back in the water, rested a few seconds and lifted it back out with his arms outstretched.

Winston steadied the camera. The fish posed nicely.

As Winston was about to shoot, the fish came to life, leaping from Victor's arms into the air and landing right in the middle of his open tackle box. The pike thrashed about, sending lures and dead fish flying.

Finally, the pike settled down and Winston gently picked him up, placed him in the water, and hooked the stringer back on the oarlock.

The boat was a disaster. "Well," Grey Wolf said grinning. "That fish gave us two nice battles."

They all laughed. It took them 20 minutes to straighten everything out. They didn't care; they would return that evening with a monster to brag about.

Chapter 9

The other boat beat us back to camp. As we pulled up, a proud Victor hoisted his monster pike out of the lake. The big fish thrashed its head and sent water spraying on us.

"How's that for a monster."

"OK, tell us the story," said Sloan.

Victor went on and on describing the battle. The look on the faces of Winston and Charlie led us to believe that Victor's story might be a wee bit exaggerated, but we had no doubts about the size of the catch.

"I'm going to have him mounted," said Victor. "Put that baby on the wall in my office. Right behind my desk."

We all had our photograph taken with Victor's fish, except Charlie, who had gone inside to fix dinner. We drank beer and told the others about Tom's encounter with the moose and afterward heard Charlie's voice, "Chow time!"

The grand meal consisted of poached whitefish and grilled trout, accompanied by Charlie's asparagus in cream sauce and a side dish of mixed brown and wild rice. Two bottles of Chateau Rothschild White Bordeaux topped off the elegant meal.

After dinner, Tom and I walked outside and contemplated the lake. A relaxing ritual we often enjoyed.

The sunset had dropped onto the horizon, and its orange-red glow covered the smooth water from the west. Soon the radiance faded and the water became more serene. The river spread out before us in a huge swirl.

Sloan and Winston joined us. We stood side by side, facing the river; and relived memories of the Albany and other streams we knew.

"These Northern Rivers kind of grow on you," said Sloan. "They hypnotize you."

"They do," said Tom, gazing in reverence at the water. "Just think, this river has been flowing for thousands of years, since the last Ice Age, 10,000 years ago, the Albany has passed this shore."

At first glance it seemed calm, but as you watched, you could see the power. Logs, ripped off the banks by the heavy current, floated by at a fast rate.

"It's cooling off," said a shivering Sloan. "It must have dropped ten degrees in the last 30 minutes."

"Time for a fire," said Winston, as he picked up short, dry branches to place in the stone pit between the cabin and the shore.

We joined him, gathering pieces of wood and twigs that had fallen off the trees during the heavy snows of winter. We never used the logs cut for the wood stove.

The stacked logs were cut to fit the cabin's woodstove. There were always fallen hardwoods like oak and maple that had been dried by the sun and wind. They kept us warm on the cold arctic nights.

Looking for campfire wood was a scavenger hunt. We all participated, except Charlie and Victor who were doing the dishes.

We gathered branches and stacked them inside the fire pit, a shallow circle of rocks, darkened by hundreds of fires set by hundreds of fishermen over the decades.

Six old tree stump seats surrounded the pit. I imagined how many stories were told here over the years. My inner reflections were halted by a shout.

"Check this out," yelled Sloan, holding an arm full of kindling and pointing at the base of a sixty-foot birch tree about forty feet from the cabin.

We walked over.

"What do you think?" Sloan said. A beaver had gnawed the tree three-quarters through about two feet off the ground.

"Wow!" Tom said, realizing that if the beaver finished his work, the tree would crash on the cabin. "We're lucky you spotted this, Sloan."

"I'd say a couple of more nibbles and we'd be in trouble," I remarked.

"I think you're right about where the tree would fall," Sloan said facing us with a broad smile.

"I guess he doesn't like people coming here," said Winston. "Get the axe Mike. I'll take care of this."

I went back to the cabin and picked up the axe. Charlie and Victor came out of the door. Charlie with a beer and Victor with a glass of Scotch. I walked back to the tree with them.

"Look at this!" I said to Charlie and Victor. "Can you imagine being wakened in the middle of the night by a tree falling through the roof?"

"No thanks," said Charlie.

"We should drop the tree nearby, but we need to be careful," said

Moonshadows

Winston.

"You're in charge," Tom said to Winston. "What do you want us to do?"

"Just stay out of the way," Winston replied. "It's bad business for a guide to drop a tree on his clients. I'll let you know when I need you fellas to push it over." Winston started chopping. About every other stroke he would look up at the tree. "I don't want this thing falling on me either," he said.

"That's what I'd call dying a stupid death. No one should die a stupid death, except stupid people," Winston added laughing.

"Do you think that beaver was trying to drop this tree on the cabin?" Charlie asked Winston. "No. Charlie. Beavers have no idea where the tree is going to fall," Winston explained. "They just like to chew them down. Why, over the years, I've found a lot of dead beavers laying under trees they were cutting."

"OK fellas," Winston said. "Get over on this side and when I say 'Go' push her over."

We put our gathered wood down and stationed ourselves, hands on the tree. "Go," he said.

We pushed hard and the birch cracked with a loud snap at its base, the sound sending all of us dancing backwards. The tree crashed onto the slope, and the bright green spring leaves shuttered as the limbs hit the ground.

"I'll chop the branches off tomorrow," said Winston.

We gathered our wood and went back to the pit. A definite chill came with the winds off the lake.

We knew how to get a fire going. We were boy scouts in our youth. Placing small, dry sticks at the bottom, we angled them up to form a tepee, so the air could rush in and around and get the heat going. After placing larger pieces of wood on top of the pile, the kindle was ready for lighting.

This is where the scouting skills of our youth left us and the need for an instantaneous blaze took over. Tom crumpled a piece of paper and lit it with his lighter. As it flamed up he placed it under the stacked twigs.

The fire started to grow, but not fast enough for Charlie, who filled a paper cup with gasoline from a fuel can by the boats. "Step back gentlemen!" Charlie yelled as he tossed it on the blaze. Whoosh! The small fire instantly became a considerable fire and we all jumped back in surprise.

"Geez, Charlie," yelled Tom. "Why did you do that?"

"I don't know, Tom. I guess I needed to get warm faster."

"Warm?" Tom said. "I feel like a friggin' marshmallow."

"The heat sure feels good," I said, rubbing my hands together.

"It warms the body and soothes the soul," added Sloan.

The fire roared now and dancing orange flames darted up and flew into the air where they disappeared. Loons called in a wild musical background. We circled the fire, just far enough away to not get burned; yet still close enough to feel the warmth of the blaze.

The darker it got, the more stars became visible. In the blackness of the wilderness you notice the stars more than you do in town. The surroundings opened our minds and our senses to the beauty of the simple things in life.

"Nature is magnificent," said Tom. "Look around us. From the stars and the water to the forest. Nature is a wonderful thing."

"And dangerous." Winston always found a way of bringing us back to reality.

"Have I ever told you about the lost fisherman?" Winston asked.

"No," said Tom.

"The incident happened here on Grassi Lake many years ago. What I tell you is a true story," Winston started with a solemn glance at us. "I was a young man in those days. I tell you now, because I am at ease with it."

Winston gazed down into the fire as he spoke. "Years ago, I was setting up camp below the rapids coming into Grassi, and my client said he wanted to get some trout for dinner." Winston continued, still staring into the blaze.

"He went, and never came back. I hunted for him for five days, until the plane came to pick us up. I did not know if the man drowned or wandered into the woods. I searched everywhere."

"What happened?" Victor inquired.

"We gave him up for dead," Winston said. "Although I still hoped he might be alive. After all, he was my responsibility. For two weeks I could not get the lost fisherman out of my mind. I even dreamed of him wandering the forests and the shores of the river."

"Then I asked Ray to fly me up here so I could spend a week searching for the man's body."

"When did this happen?" I asked.

"Back in 1990," he said. "In the spring, early June. The nights still cold, and the days filled with mosquitoes and black flies." Winston stirred the fire with a stick and sparks floated into the air.

"As Ray prepared to land on Grassi, we saw this creature crawling along the shore. It resembled a bear at first, all huddled over, and dark. We circled and came in low and saw it was a man, moving very slow on all fours.

"We landed and Ray taxied the plane toward shore. What we found was beyond comprehension. It was the fisherman who wandered away almost three weeks before.

"His clothes were torn and tattered, his face and hands swollen by the bites of mosquitoes and black flies, and his beard was full of dried blood. He endured more than any of us could imagine, yet he still lived. We carried him to the plane and flew him to the hospital in Thunder Bay."

Winston reminded us of something he told us on every trip. "Never take a shortcut," he said, pointing to each of us circling the fire.

"What happened to him?" Charlie asked.

"He took what he thought was a shortcut and walked in huge circles. He knew he was lost, of course, but he could not find water. He told us later he became confused and could not even find his direction for three days because of clouds.

"He told us he caught some spawning suckers in a stream he damned up."

"Did he have matches?" Victor asked.

"No," said Winston. "He ate everything raw and that made him sick. He also killed some spruce hens by throwing rocks at them. He remembered you can eat the inside bark of the birch tree; he barely survived on this until we came upon him."

Winston picked up more wood and threw the small branches into the fire. "He was a madman when we found him, but brave, a survivor. He died of a heart attack climbing a mountain five years ago."

"There are lessons in Winston's story," Tom reminded us.

"Never leave the river and always have a compass."

"And matches, preferably waterproof ones," added Victor. "After all, if you are going to get lost you should still be able to enjoy a good cigar."

We briefly laughed. Then the silence returned.

We all gazed at the fire. It was hypnotic. It always is.

"How about a short canoe trip down the lake?" Tom said, poking me gently in the arm. "It's a beautiful night and we should take advantage of the nice weather."

"Just a brief one," I replied. "I'm tired."

"I'll go with you," Winston said, "but I'll be the designated paddler. You've both been drinking and I don't want you getting drowned or lost."

We smiled. I was glad he was coming with us.

Charlie, Victor and Sloan stayed close to the fire as we launched the canoe into the darkness.

The moon was bright and nearly full. It made for a clear night. We went at an easy pace as Winston quietly paddled us upstream against the heavy current.

Close to midnight, everything was obscure except a faint glow along the horizon that silhouetted the shoreline trees against the fading sky. No one had spoken for quite awhile.

The current of the Albany rippled around us as we approached the upstream rapids. At the edge of the whitewater, we turned around to head back to camp.

I was sitting on the middle seat gazing up at the sky. Tom was laid out on his back with his head resting on a seat cushion in the bow of the canoe. He also looked up into the night. All was silent except for the sound of the river.

As it got even darker, the sky became mesmerizing.

More stars kept appearing, faintly at first and then brighter than I had ever seen them before or since. Soon there were countless stars sparkling from one end of the horizon to the other, big stars, and radiant stars, thousands of stars.

Then the sky became even more magnificent. Northern Lights, the Aurora Borealis, burst across the horizon with pale blue strands, then they became more numerous and spread as far as one could see. They started as bands shooting up and soon turned to giant waves of ribbon candy covering the sky all around us.

The ribbons of pastel green, red, pink, violet, and pale gold waved in the night sky. They pulsated from the horizon up to the zenith. It was a dazzling display.

Winston continued toward the cabin. The only sound was the

swishing of his paddle in the fast water. Even the loons were quiet now.

"What a show," I said to Tom. "I've seen the Northern Lights many times, but not like this. This is beyond words."

Tom smiled in agreement, as we gazed into the firmament.

"You know," he said. "This is the most amazing, beautiful and peaceful night of my life. There is magic in the sky."

Then Winston, who had been silent for the entire canoe trip, stopped paddling, stretched out his arms toward the sky, and spoke. "These are my ancestors dancing for us," he said. Then he began paddling again.

Tom sat up, and he and I looked at one another.

"What do you mean?" I asked.

"They dance to entertain us," Winston said. "They know our life down here has much misery, so they dance to make us happy. They are with God."

"So you believe in God?" Tom asked him.

"Yes," said Winston. "I have met God."

"Met Him?" Tom said.

We listened attentively to the coming answer. Grey Wolf stopped paddling and stared at us. "Yes. When I was a boy of 14, I asked my father how I could meet God. He told me that God was everywhere and I met him every day.

A few days later, I was walking a shoreline trail to check some traps when I met an old woman. She was sitting on a log weaving a basket.

I sat down next to her and offered her some dried meat. The old woman accepted it gratefully and smiled at me."

He paddled a few more strokes to keep our momentum going.

"I gave her a drink of water. Again, she smiled at me. We spent the day together talking about the woods and the animals. She knew much about the animals. As the evening approached, I got up to leave, but before I went far, I turned around to thank her for the knowledge she gave me, but she was gone. When I arrived home, my father was curious about the smile on my face."

"What did you do today that made you so happy?"

"I shared a meal with God," I answered.

"With God?"

"Yes," I said, "and he is much older than I expected, and a woman!"

Tom and I smiled.

"My answer made my father happy. He told me how proud he was of me to aid the old woman."

"That's a beautiful story," Tom said.

"It is a true one," said Winston. "My father taught me we are the sum of all the people we meet in life. How they treat us and how we treat them is what we become. My father was a good man."

The night fell silent.

Chapter 10

The morning came clear and cold, with a springtime Ontario chill in the air.

Getting up, I stoked wood in the stove to warm the cabin, and made coffee in the large pot. I walked outside. A light dusting of snow covered the ground.

Birch, poplar, pines and tamarack dominated the shoreline. I heard the rapids where the river enters the lake, and the roar of the whitewater falls at the outlet.

Looking out over the wilderness, I realized the difference between living in the city and the North. In the wild you are surrounded by life. Everything is alive, the ground you walk on, the sky above your head, the river that flows, the treetops swaying in the breeze, the sounds of animals, seen and unseen. Life surrounds you.

Back home, in the "civilized" world, you walk on concrete and drive on asphalt. There, you rarely thought of looking up at the stars and the moon, because the city lights make the heavens hard to see. Noise encloses you: cars, trucks, busses, horns, phones ringing, and more. Here, only you and nature make the sound.

On most days, you wake up to the call of loons and the slaps of beaver tails. In the spring the grouse are close. The males drum their wings and strut around the cabin as if they want to mate with it.

Flying in, as you circle the lake, the first thing you notice is the forested shore is littered with large trees, many of them birch and poplar jagged and twisted on the ground. The wreckage continues up into the woods for 200 feet at various spots.

What could cause this you think? The answer soon dawns on you, beaver. Beaver, once virtually extinct in Northern Ontario, are back. Trapping had wiped them out. Then the government of Canada decided to restock the beaver. As the beaver were reestablished the fur business died. No fur business, no trappers. No trappers, more beaver. Today, the beaver control the North, not only on the Albany, but all the rivers, streams and lakes.

I walked back into the warm cabin. The aroma of the fresh brewed coffee filled the room. Sleeping bags began to move around in a restless sort of ritual. One by one heads appeared and peeked about, checking to see if the coffee was ready.

The occupants of the bags were gathering courage to venture forth out of their womb-like warmth into the cool air.

I turned the fire on under the iron griddle.

Sloan got out of his cocoon, stood up and did about five seconds worth of stretches.

"Want some coffee?" I asked.

"Do you need an answer?" Sloan said with a smile.

"How many glugs?"

"Two good ones," he said.

I tilted the bottle of Bailey's Irish Cream until the liquid made two distinct bubbling sounds into his waiting cup.

"Thanks," he said.

"Weather looks good."

"I agree," Sloan said gazing out of the window, his hands clutching the steaming cup. "What's for breakfast?"

"How about blueberry pancakes?"

I threw some drops of water on the grill plate covering two of the burners on the stove. They sizzled and danced across the surface. The grill was hot and ready for the batter.

I made the cakes small, three at a time. As they cooked on one side I'd add fresh blueberries and flip them cautiously in order to retain the artistic beauty of the blueberries already tucked into the batter.

"Those look tasty," Sloan said, looking over my shoulder.

"They're not tasty," I said. "They're unbelievable."

Sloan sat down at the table and leafed through an old issue of Field & Stream.

"I hear the fish calling," I said, "life is wonderful."

"Not always," said Sloan.

"What do you mean? Are you getting philosophical already?"

"I don't know," said Sloan. "There are OK days and bad days." He hesitated. "On the bad days I walk away from life, sort of escape, helps me keep my sanity."

"There are many ways to approach it," I said. "When life treats you bad, I believe you have to face your problems head on."

Sloan took a puff on his cigar, tilted his head back and blew a whiff of smoke straight up into the air, then stared at me. "Why bother?" Sloan said. "I've found it's better to ignore the situation. Makes everything easier to cope with, don't you think?"

"No. There are only three ways to cope with any situation. One is to run away. Another is to hide. And the third is to deal with it."

"The first two seem the best," said Sloan.

"Do you really believe that?"

"After all these years, I think so," he replied.

I thought about his answer and figured my friend was another victim of what I call, 'Who you are is who you are,' or my wife's version, which is, "When people tell you who they are, believe them."

At an early age, someone taught Sloan, or somehow he learned, when conflict arose you avoided the problem. The problem is, that way the problem is never resolved.

He believed evasion made him safe, kept him from losing the battle. But, escaping also prevented him from winning.

"Sloan, all you're doing is hiding if you run away from a conflict. And, even if you hide, you might have to face the same situation again."

"Not always," he told me. "Sometimes I get peace."

"Your peace comes at a price. If you spend your life running and hiding you never win. You also allow and encourage the person who created the conflict to pass it on to you and others. If you believe in your heart a person is wrong, you must say so. There is only one way to win, and that is to stand and fight."

"Man, this is way too serious of a conversation," said a wide-awake Charlie from his sleeping bag. "I may as well get up and straighten you guys out."

Charlie worked slowly out of his bag, sat up, and placed his feet on the floor. "Jesus!" Charlie screamed, quickly lifting his feet up. "The floor is frozen."

"The heat's coming," I said. "I've only been up about a half hour. It takes a while you know."

Charlie snuggled back into his cocoon.

"I've got to get some feeling back in my feet."

"Don't you want some Bailey's?" Sloan said, waving his cup in front of Charlie's face. "Come and get it."

"I'll wait," said Charlie. "You know the sooner you fall behind, the

Robert B. Gregg

more time you'll have to catch up."
    We thought about his statement, but not for long.
    Charlie stayed in his bag and waited for the cabin to warm.

Chapter 11

A frosting of snow still hung in the trees, edging the bright green springtime leaves in white.

"Time to take a dump," Victor announced as he rose from the breakfast table. "Did anyone bring anything good to read?"

"I've got the 'Meditations of Marcus Aurelius,'" said Sloan, "but that may be a bit too intellectual for you."

"Give me the book," said Victor, amused. "There is still hope for the ignorant of the world."

Sloan dug the small book out of his duffle and handed it to Victor.

"If I'm not back in an hour, come and wake me up. By the way, did anyone stock toilet paper in the outhouse?"

"There's a good supply," said Charlie.

"The soft stuff, Charmin?" Victor inquired.

"Charmin," said Charlie. "We don't use that cheap stuff."

Victor smiled and walked out the door, book in hand. Walking around to the back of the cabin, he followed the well-worn trail to relief.

The path had witnessed thousands of trips over the many years. Some people in a hurry, some not, the brave ones even came in the middle of the night. Many never made the trek all the way, and just stopped and peed alongside the trail.

The outhouse stood majestically at the end of the path. Each wall was a sheet of 4' by 8' plywood with a hinged door on the front. It had two small, screened windows, one on each side for cross-ventilation. The interior consisted of a wooden bench seat with a hole cut in it. A flat, porous, plywood roof was peaked on top.

There were holes in the walls where the knots had fallen out. Outside, encircled by a thick stand of black spruce, the building was covered with fungus, moss and lichen. The walls were naturally stained a dark green.

Inside, keeping you company, several varieties of spiders, along with the usual mosquitoes and black flies. Victor passed the time studying the intricate web designs and the bodies of insects captured by the resident arachnids, especially a wolf spider, aka 'the big guy' who controlled the center spring area inside the door.

The hole, covered by a plastic seat and lid cover, was in the middle of the board and, when seated, on the left rolls of toilet paper, some wet, some dry, depending on their position under the leaking roof.

On the right side, magazines were strewn everywhere. There were two very old, well-used copies of Field & Stream, along with copies of Outdoor Life, In-Fisherman, Sports Afield, Gray's Sporting Journal and Cigar Aficionado.

Victor sat down on the bench and faced the door. Emblazoned on it in black, felt-tipped marker was: "Hey You! Yes You! You only had one cup of coffee and you've been in here for an hour. Put the magazine down, and MOVE IT! People are waiting."

Victor grinned at the saying, opened the book by Marcus Aurelius, and got comfortable, or as comfortable as one could get in such a place.

The book began, *"From my grandfather Verus I learned good morals and the government of my temper. From the reputation and remembrance of my father, modesty and manly character. From my mother, piety and generosity, and abstinence, not only from evil deeds, but even from evil thoughts, and further, simplicity in my way of living."*

Being rich, Victor found the beginning intriguing. He relaxed and read on.

Moonshadows

Chapter 12

The sun rose in a blue sky. The air was warm. Winston motored up the shore with Charlie in the middle and me in the bow. We started the angling at the incoming rapids where I had fished the day before.

I prefer getting into the water and wading, because I become easily bored in a boat. I've always found it too confining. I have a restless nature and a need to move.

We began the day by portaging the upstream set of rapids. We dragged the boat through a swamp, pushing it into the rapids. I occupied the bow, holding onto some shoreline brush to keep the boat steady while Charlie got in the middle. Winston entered and started the motor. He nodded his head to me to let go of the brush, and I climbed over the side. We cautiously moved through the rapids against the heavy current. I had brought along my Go Pro camera to film our trip.

A massive boulder caused the fast flow to split, causing a smooth stretch of calm between the streams of angry water at our sides. Winston slid into the calm behind the rock and, using the motor, held the boat out of the current.

"Cast along the edges of the fast water," he told us. "Use a good-sized silver spinner. Some monster pike live here."

I put the camera away. We started casting. I tossed left. Charlie right.

In a matter of moments Charlie hooked a huge 'Najobi,' (Na-job-ee) the Cree name for pike. The fish hit hard, raced into the maelstrom, jumped and the spinner came flying back at us, striking the side of the boat hard.

"Wow! That's a great start!" said Charlie.

"A great start is a fish on the stringer," I said teasing him.

Several casts later, we struck gold. We enjoyed a double-header, two fish on at the same time. Charlie's hit first, a few seconds later I hooked one. We landed both fish and put them on the stringer. Charlie's fish a grand forty-one inches long, mine thirty-nine.

We hooked up with more than a dozen pike that morning between thirty-five and forty-one inches in length, bringing half to net and returning all but one, Charlie's monster.

The weather warmed and Charlie drank beer after beer. I noticed his never-ending grin getting wider and wider. He was "shitfaced."

A little while later, Winston took us to fish for trout in some quiet water below a set of shallow rapids. We pulled our fly rods out and waded along the shore while our guide sat on a log and watched.

We were using five weight rods with six-pound leader and fishing stonefly nymph patterns for brook trout. Canadian trout love stoneflies. Casting upstream and letting the fly free-drift along the bottom in the fast current seemed the most productive technique. We used small pieces of Styrofoam as strike indicators. Setting the hooks instantly on strike was the only way to get a hookup.

Charlie was upstream from me when I heard him yell excitedly.

"Mike. Get over here quick! I need your help. There are hundreds of trout rising in this pool and I can't get them to hit."

I waded ashore and hustled to the spot.

"Look at them," he said pointing to the water. I gazed at the pool and started laughing.

"Those aren't rises," I said. "It's raining!" The smooth, glimmering sun was shining, but a small, single black cloud drifted over us causing a light drizzle to occur only in front of Charlie.

Charlie stared at the water, turned to me and said, "That's why I couldn't get them to hit. Man, I think I've had too many beers."

We saw Winston coming towards us.

"Don't tell Winston."

As I agreed to his request, the rain stopped.

"Want to catch some even bigger fish?" Winston said to us during the lull in the action.

"Sure," Charlie said. I agreed. We walked together back to the boat, excited as little kids.

Winston powered us upstream, and we stopped, pulled out the spinning rods again and fished for a while in a wide, swirling pool formed by the end of a powerful whitewater chute. We spent a half hour casting without a hit.

"Nothing here," said Charlie.

"They're here," said a reassuring Winston as he motored over to a ledge near the bank of the river. "Why don't you fellas get out and fish along the side of this ledge. The big ones like hiding right next to it. I'll be right back."

Winston dropped Charlie and me off on the limestone ledge at the

Moonshadows

base of a waterfall. He handed me the stringer of fish.

"Take care of these," he said. I wondered why he didn't just keep them attached to the gunwale of the boat.

The river narrowed here and the whole force of its flow came crashing through a set of horrendous rapids.

"I thought we were going to portage and fish upriver," I said.

"The fishing is OK here," Winston said to me, as he got ready to push off.

"Do me a favor," he added. "I'm going across to portage above the falls and I'm going to run the falls and the rapids. Would you film me running the rapids? I've never done this before. Fact is no one has ever run these rapids before. I'll wave my arms to signal my start."

Before either of us could answer, Winston left and motored across to the shallow eddy where he could take out and portage up and over the right side of the cascading cataract. We felt abandoned.

Our outlook from the ledge seemed too low to get a good view of Winston's folly. We quickly scrambled up to the top of a large granite outcrop 20 feet above the water to get a better panorama. The rocks were wicked slick from the melting snow and brief rain. We found the climbing difficult.

A few minutes later, we surveyed the river to film what we thought would be our guide's death.

When Winston finished the portage he hand-lined the boat through some wicked fast shallow water. Reaching the edge of the rapids, he flopped over the side into the boat, and gunned the engine against the raging waters.

It took him a couple of minutes of slow running and maneuvering to reach the pool above the foaming water that led over the falls.

Winston turned the boat, faced down river and stood up with his right hand on the motor handle. The boat held for a moment as Winston gazed downstream, seeking a path through the maelstrom. He abruptly sat down, waved to us, and the whitewater adventure began.

Bang! Ten yards into the challenge Winston flew off his seat, disappearing into the bottom of the boat as it ricocheted off a huge boulder. Partially hidden under the waves, the boulder was obviously not part of his plan. He quickly scrambled up, grabbed the motor handle and yelled "Yahoo." His scream overcoming the roar of the rapids.

Usually quite reserved, Winston continued to grin and yell his way through the rocks and the waves.

"Yahoo."

Often the bow would drop below the water, then pop up as the boat took flight, and slammed down hard into the next white wave. On and on he went.

"Yahoo. Yahoo."

Every once in a while he would ricochet off a boulder and the boat would serpentine out of control. Well into the rapids he joined the final narrow chute where the whole river surged into a giant white wave. He attacked the foam.

As we watched, he vanished. There were no more yahoos.

"What now?" Charlie said to me. The situation didn't look good. Our guide had gone under and not come up. Then, like Lazarus rising from the dead, Winston, and the boat, rose from the waves, popping up like a cork below the falls, some 200 feet downstream.

He had conquered the unconquerable rapids.

We rushed down to the rock shelf below the falls to meet him. Winston motored the boat up onto the ledge. His shirt and pants stuck to his body and his hair was pasted against his head, he resembled a drowned bear. The boat was half full of water.

"A big yahoo," he said to me as he got out and handed the bow rope to Charlie. "Did you get that on film?"

"I sure did!" I told him.

"I didn't think I was going to make it. Thought I'd drown in the damn Albany like my brother."

I knew him to be tough, but this is the first time I saw him foolhardy.

"That was dangerous," I told him.

"No kidding," he said.

He wore out the camera battery that night, watching his amazing death defying run, over, and over, and over.

Chapter 13

We met back at camp for dinner. Charlie's chance to brag. He talked incessantly about the gigantic pike he caught.

"The biggest pike of my life," he said, "and I lost some others that were monsters."

I backed up his story.

"Say Charlie, I hate to cut you off, but we have some starving guys gathered here. We'll start a bonfire out here, and you get dinner going," Tom said pointing to the cabin.

Chef Charlie got the hint. "OK," he said. "I know you guys are jealous, but you'll have to get used to my success, because this expertise of mine is going to go on all week. But before I go in, I'd like to give you old farts a quiz to find out if you have Alzheimer's."

"Just because we're all over forty doesn't make us old farts," said Victor, piling sticks in the fire pit.

"Well," said Charlie. "I didn't say you Have Alzheimer's."

We gathered around.

"Exercise of the brain is as important as exercise of the muscles," said Charlie. "As we grow older, we must keep mentally alert. The saying 'If you don't use it, you lose it,' also applies to the brain, so listen up. I'm going to determine if you guys are losing it or are still OK. Are you ready?"

"Sure," said Sloan with a grin. We all agreed.

"OK, relax and clear your mind," said Charlie "What do you put in a toaster?"

"Bread," we all answered.

"Good," said Charlie. "I thought I'd start you off with an easy one so you didn't hurt yourselves."

"OK, say "silk" five times.

We all said silk five times.

Now spell "silk."

We all went S-I-L-K.

What do cows drink?

"Milk," I quickly answered. The others were silent.

"One down," said Charlie. "Cows drink water. Your brain is overstressed already. You're out of the competition."

Robert B. Gregg

Embarrassed and eliminated, I started the campfire while the others played on. My quick response eliminated me early. I do the same thing when I watch Jeopardy.

Charlie continued, "If a red house is made from red bricks, and a blue house is made from blue bricks, and a pink house is made from pink bricks, and a black house is made from black bricks, what is a green house made from?"

"Glass," everyone said.

"Wow, you are a sharp group. Except for this guy," he said pointing to me.

"Without using a calculator, you are driving a bus from Chicago to Detroit. In Chicago, 17 people get on the bus. In Kalamazoo, six people get off the bus and nine people get on. In Lansing, two people get off and four get on. In Ann Arbor, 11 people get off and 16 people get on. In Dearborn, three people get off and five people get on. You arrive in Detroit."

Everyone seemed in deep thought, but ready to answer.

"What was the name of the bus driver?"

The entire group exhibited a blank look on their faces. They stared at one another. Charlie waited, and then broke the silence.

"For crying out loud. Don't you recall your own name? You're the driver. Remember, I started by saying, 'You're driving a bus from Chicago to Detroit.'"

"Go fix dinner," said Tom, laughing along with the rest of us. We were Charlie's victims again.

"Poached pike and trout tonight gentlemen," Charlie said. "Dinner will be ready in an hour and a half." Speed had no importance to Charlie, perfection did, and we loved the outcome.

The roaring fire attracted us, like all men are drawn to campfires. The flames functioned as our social gathering place every evening, and this night would prove no different.

The sun turned a strange dark, blood red as it started to set in the clear sky.

"Looks ominous," said Sloan. "I've never seen a sunset quite like that."

"It does look strange," Tom concurred.

"The river is high," said Sloan to Winston. "Tomorrow will be a

Moonshadows

challenge. Do you still want to portage the falls and go downstream?"

"The falls won't be a problem if we are cautious and take our time," said Winston.

"OK," said Tom. "Down the river we go. Rapids. Adventure. Trophy trout. Everything we came up here for. To the challenge of the river," he said, raising his beer in a toast. We lifted our drinks in response.

"How's your cousin James doing?" I asked Winston.

"I didn't know you knew James," he replied.

"Sure. He guided us years ago on our first trip to the Albany. We stayed at Makokibatan Lodge, I believe. An interesting fellow."

"You speak kindly," said Winston. "James and I grew up together."

"Where?" I asked.

"On the Albany," said Winston. "On an island between here and Fort Hope."

"I've never asked you, but what was it like growing up?"

"My dad trapped and fished for sturgeon. He used gill nets. Took me with him sometimes."

"Where did you go to school?" Victor asked.

"We started government school in Nakina at the age of nine. Spent three years there, except summers when I helped my mom and dad.

"My dad was the most honorable man you could know. He would give you the shirt off his back. My mom used to share food with the fishermen when they ran out."

"You're talking about the early 60's right?" Sloan asked.

"Yes," said Winston. "When I was a child, we still lived in tents. Life treated us well. As I got older, I had my own trap line. I'd set my traps near our camp. When I was small, every morning, in winter, my dad would put an animal in one of my traps to encourage me to check my lines."

Winston hesitated and searched deep into his memories. We all stared into the flames and waited.

"He got tired of it eventually and told me the truth. After that I needed to catch my own."

"Tell us more," said Tom.

"One summer a bear kept coming around our camp watching my brothers and sisters and me. My dad had to shoot the beast."

"I'll bet you have a lot of great animal stories," I said.

69

"Oh yes," said Winston. "We always had animals as pets. We got a new pet beaver from my dad every spring for a while. You knew they were ready to leave when they started eating the table legs. One time dad gave us two bear cubs. They are just like dogs. They slept huddled up close to the wood stove. They left in the fall."

"Sounds like a wonderful childhood," said Tom.

"Yes," said Winston. "We also got a new crow every spring. The bird would live with us until fall, then leave. There were always more crows in our area the next spring, usually nesting nearby."

"How many brothers and sisters do you have?" I asked.

"Three of each," said Winston. "I am the oldest. Most of the Indians in this region are Catholics."

"Are you Catholic?" Tom asked.

"Yes," said Winston, "Catholic Indians have an ever-present God who believe the woods are full of spirits. Spirits with voices that influence our everyday life."

We listened intently.

"Most of the spirits are brooding and evil," he said. "These hold supremacy."

"That's pretty scary stuff," said Victor.

"Some believe that headless skeletons run the forest at night," said Winston, staring at Sloan and slowly waving his extended arms.

"Whoa," said Sloan. "Winston my man, you are scaring the hell out of me"

Winston smiled a strange smile. He enjoyed telling stories and trying to scare us, especially Sloan.

"In some back eddies of the river, Sloan, are dead men who swim only at the full of the moon."

"Dead men?" Sloan asked.

"The Windigo," said Winston. "They are half-human, flesh-eating creatures who scour the shores of the lakes and rivers looking for those who sleep carelessly without fire. They make sleeping in some areas a thing of horror."

Sloan seemed to believe the story.

"Say, don't take this too seriously," I said to him.

"Winston, you can tell a tale or two," said Sloan.

"These are not tales," Winston insisted.

"There are many spirits here, now, around us, both good and bad. Under this very ground we stand on is Hayowatha, not the one of your poem, but the wise prophet and gentle soul who calls the animals little brothers. He is a prophet who works only for good. He is not to be feared. He wakes once a year in the fall and releases the Hunting Winds and opens the Four Way Lodge.

"His spirit moves through the woods to those he hopes to save. He goes about the land surrounded by his furred and feathered friends and is guarded by a pack of great wolves. We know when he has awakened because we hear the cry of the phantom wolf pack and the calls of the phantom beaver.

"Every night we hear the wolves and the beaver around these waters. How can you be sure which night is the night of the Hunting Winds?" Tom asked.

"It is the night you choose," said Winston, pointing to his chest. "You know it in your heart."

We drank our beer; dinner was still a long ways off.

"So what about James? What's he doing these days?" I asked again.

"He's a big mucky-muck up at Fort Hope," said Winston.

Fort Hope is an Indian settlement on the Albany, and a former Hudson Bay trading post.

"James is an important man," said Winston. "A big cheese. He traps this area in the winter."

"Does he stay here or the cabin across the lake?"

"Neither. He has a trapper's cabin not far from here, hidden from the shore, not seen from the lake."

Then I remembered. "I have been to James' cabin. Years ago. He showed me the pelt stretchers and traps."

"I'd like to see this place," said a curious Victor. "How far is it from here?"

"Less than a mile, but the trail is hidden by heavy brush and hasn't been used since last winter. James doesn't want anyone to stumble onto his winter home."

"Can we check this out?" said Tom.

"Sure," said Winston. "Now would be a good time. The weather is clear."

We all agreed.

Robert B. Gregg

"Dress warm," our guide instructed. "Put on jackets. The temperature will drop as soon as the sun sets and we will be gone for close to an hour."

We left the camp following Winston like puppies follow their mom, excited about our little adventure. Charlie stayed behind working on dinner and keeping an eye on the campfire.

The sun dropped to the horizon behind the trees and you could feel the chill air on your face as the wind picked up.

"The weather is changing fast," said a worried Winston, looking up at the sky.

The journey started along the trail to the outhouse. Just as we reached the outhouse, Winston turned left and started moving several pieces of deadfall out of the way. "Help me out here," he told us. "The trail is hidden behind these branches."

As we tossed the brush aside, the path became obvious. "Stay with me," said Winston. "Remember, we have to camouflage the trail on our return." Single file, with our guide in the lead, we moved into the darkening forest. The woods were shadowy and foreboding, and we loved the feeling.

The trail began flat and narrow. The trees grew tight together. We traveled at a steady pace. We could still hear the upstream rapids. Every once in a while we would glimpse the setting sun, then the trees would get thick again and blot out the glow. Several times we struck off to the side to avoid deadfall.

As our eyes adjusted to the darker forest, we noticed more animal tracks. In the North, animals, more than humans, make the trails. Tracks are everywhere.

We ascended a small hill that gave us a clear view of the lake. We spotted two of the men from the other camp, across the lake, fishing in a boat, close to the opposite shore. I wondered if they had caught anything.

The lake glowed as if on fire as the sunset's remarkable colors cast long shadows on the water. It was the strangest sunset I had ever seen.

Soon, the trail entered the dimming woods again and became hard to discern. We constantly went up and down and the brush kept getting thicker. "Watch out for the spirits, Sloan," said Winston with a menacing chuckle. Sloan showed no reaction.

He led us on through the maze of thickets, brush and dense forest without a hesitation in his step. Then he became the teacher. He was

Moonshadows

always teaching us something about the North.

"Walking trails is a pleasant thing," he said stopping. "Often exciting and peaceful at the same time.

"Years ago, I met a lone wolf on a night like this," said Winston as he pointed to a birch tree near the path. "He gazed at me and I at him. I felt a connection. I would like to meet him again some day.

"When you are alone, the trail is your entertainment. It's where you gather knowledge about the woods and the wildlife around you.

"Long hikes can test your character, because the trail demands awareness, and sometimes endurance. If you are careless, you can become lost and pay the ultimate price. "Lose the trail and you could be harmed. Stay the trail and you are always rewarded."

Our guide turned and continued on at a quick pace.

My thinking distracted me and my left foot plunged into a hollow in the muskeg and I fell forward knocking Victor down with me. Everyone stopped. Victor and I stared at each other in the dusk of the forest.

"Jesus," said Victor. "Are you all right?" We got to our feet.

"Yea. I think so," I said brushing myself off. "Just daydreaming. Went through the muskeg."

Winston looked at me and shook his head, disappointed at my clumsiness. "Tomorrow we will have a class on how to walk trails," he said with a grin.

We walked a gradual downhill that curved and forced us deeper into the woods.

The hike became quiet now, except for the shuffling of our feet through the leaves and twigs on the forest floor. Trees filed by us. We no longer felt the chill. The exercise brought warmth to our bodies. All around the forest continued silent. We were surrounded by scattered spruce and birch stands and heavy underbrush and deadfall.

Suddenly ahead, we heard a crashing, cracking sound. "Get behind a tree!" Winston yelled back at us. Then we perceived a massive black beast, weighing half a ton, with a cumbersome head and big bulging eyes, and headed our way down the trail. We stood stunned like deer in the headlights.

A bull moose, his ears laid back, charged right at us. He swung his massive horns from side to side, catching branches and knocking down small rotten trees. The pounding of his hooves sounded like a freight train

Robert B. Gregg

coming through the forest. As he approached, he snorted and the hair bristled on his back.

We scrambled to hopeful safety.

The moose took big, long strides running past us without hesitation.

We only came out of hiding when we heard the thumps of his hooves fading into the distance.

The panic ended as swiftly as it started. My knees shook.

"What a thrill," said Winston, smiling from behind a pine tree.

"I about crapped my pants," said Tom.

"He must have been getting a drink at the lake and we caught him by surprise," said Winston. "Bulls use the same trails over and over. They go down to the river every morning and late every evening. This is the only time of the day when you can surprise them."

I wasn't sure who was surprised the most, but I believe we all were, including our able Indian guide. By fortunate circumstance, we escaped unharmed.

"We're lucky it wasn't a cow with newly-born calves," said Winston. "She probably would have stuck around and caused some big problems."

We continued our evening hike, passing from dark to sunset shadows and back again.

A big bull moose racing through the woods is an awesome sight. Moose are the Northern Indians' main food. A good size moose can feed a family for a big part of a year.

Life is tough in the North and moose provides the protein that breaks up the monotony of store-bought food that comes at a high-price and is often hard to get.

Winston stopped and asked us to help him build a footbridge across a feeder stream with broken limbs. When done, we gingerly crossed the bridge, which moved ever so slightly under our feet.

After the moose incident we listened more intently, each of us peeking around the person in front of him to get a better glimpse of the path ahead.

We headed toward the shore again, down to a low spot and then back up into the woods. The trail meandered in and out of the trees, taking in everything the forest offered.

Climbing steadily now, our group moved up onto a thick, forested bluff that overlooked the lake. Winston picked up the pace. "Almost there

Moonshadows

men," he said to us without turning around.

"Great," said Victor, breathing heavily.

The trapper's cabin, a low-lying log structure stood before us, well hidden in forested opening. The cabin looked the same to me as 20 years before. The entire hut stood just over five feet high and was made up of logs, limbs and branches of every shape and size, and chinked together with mud, tundra and muskeg. The trees were close by, almost touching the cabin with their branches. The place blended in with the woods.

You couldn't see the cabin from the lake even if you knew the location. A thick stand of spruce stood between the cabin and the water, and heavy brush grew between the trees.

The door wasn't locked. They never are in the north. We opened the door and the rusty hinges squeaked. A little light came in with us as we entered one by one.

Inside we found a single bunk and a small table with one chair. The walls were covered with dozens of traps of various sizes for bear, lynx, marten, fox and others. Most of them, however, were designed for beaver.

Piles of wooden pelt stretchers lay near the wall. A woodstove like the one in our cabin was near the door. A small cupboard held some cans of food and several books. A Bible lay open on the table. A washbasin sat on a shelf.

In the far corner, away from the door, stood a double-barreled, 12-gauge shotgun. A half-filled case of slugs and some loaded shells sat against the near wall.

I walked over to the gun. "James is a trusting soul to leave his shotgun here," I said, examining the weapon.

"Why?" Winston said matter-of-factly. "Those who live off the land would never steal. We have an unwritten law. No one would dare take the gun who did not need the weapon as a matter of life or death?"

My statement embarrassed me.

The cabin had one window, a slot two feet wide by six inches high that could be closed with a piece of sliding wood. We walked around examining things.

"What a place," commented Victor. "Man, to live like this, alone, all winter. Wow."

"I've trapped alone for many winters," Winston informed Victor.

75

"Trapping is hard work, but I'd rather run a trap line than do anything else."

"I meant no offense," said Victor.

"None taken."

"This cabin looks really old," commented Sloan.

"The cabin has been here since beyond my years," Winston said. "My uncle discovered the place almost 60 years ago. He shot a moose from his canoe and came ashore to follow the wounded beast.

"He found a pile of human bones covered in rags next to the fire pit. The man had been dead for years. The door lay open. Porcupines had half eaten the furniture and mice had taken over. My uncle buried the man and repaired the cabin."

"James' father?" I asked.

"Yes," said Winston. "He is a better man than his son."

I thought about Winston's remark briefly and decided not to inquire further as to why he deemed his uncle a better man than his cousin James.

We continued our investigation into a trapper's life as a pack of wolves began calling in the deep woods.

"They do that when the moon is near full," said Winston referring to the howls. Then the howling stopped.

The evening fell silent, except for a gust of wind that whistled through the trees.

"How often does James use this place?" said Sloan.

"James comes here when the geese head south in the fall," Winston said. "Usually late August or early September. A canoe is hidden in the brush down near shore. James uses it to hunt during the fall. When things freeze up, he traps. He runs his trap lines on snowshoes. He stays until the river starts to break up in the spring."

We wandered around the cabin and the camp for a few more minutes.

"I'm as hungry as a seagull at a gravel pit," Tom said. "Let's head back."

"And let's hope we don't run into any more moose," Victor added.

Chapter 14

The day started ugly. Black clouds covering the sky and darkening the lake hid the sun. The morning broke with a sense of dread.

We peeked out of the window, and were tempted to go back to sleep. A light snow had fallen over night. The grass in front of the camp was dusted in white. It was cold and damp. The cabin was silent. The crew, tired from the first two days of adventure, was slow to wake up.

I too was a reluctant riser, but knew my duty. I moved slowly out of my sleeping bag, got the wood stove going, and crawled back in, waiting for the cabin to warm. A half hour later, I ventured forth again to make coffee and start breakfast.

I started scrambling eggs in one pan and searing bacon in the other. As the food finished, I placed the bacon into the big iron skillet with the eggs and put the skillet into the warm oven. The mixing odors would bring the others to life.

"Smells good," came a muffled voice. Charlie peeked out from his cocoon. He appeared rough, unkempt. He got up and went straight for the refrigerator. He opened the door and stared in.

"Where's the beer?"

"It's 7 o'clock in the morning," I said with a snicker.

"I didn't ask for the time. I asked where the beer was."

"In the cooler on the porch," I said as I motioned toward the door.

Most people would have been annoyed by Charlie's line of questioning, but we knew him, and loved him, and expected such an inquiry at 7 o'clock in the morning.

We finished breakfast, put on our rainwear and loaded our fishing tackle in our backpacks. We would probably do some portaging today.

The wind blew hard from the Northeast, a very bad sign. "Get all the wood inside the screened-in porch," said Winston. "We may need more than we think before the week is up."

A warm cabin, hot breakfast and the smell of coffee eventually awakened the dead. Everyone moved slowly, reluctant to face the day. We put on layers of clothes, starting with breathable polypropylene next to our skin, regular warm clothes and waterproof jackets and pants.

We finished and went outside.

"Geez!" Victor shouted. "Hang on. I'm going back in for a heavier jacket."

A bitter cold wind hit us as we left the dock in two separate boats to head down river. Three of us would fish one side of the river. The others would fish the opposite shore. We were all after trout. We planned an all-day trip with three portages, the first, to avoid a short but wicked waterfall, the other two, to go around risky rapids.

We hoped to return before it got dark and dangerous.

The river ran even higher than the day before. The current was swift, strong and wicked from heavy rains upstream. Two miles from camp, we approached the fast, slick water about a quarter mile above the waterfall.

Tom, Charlie and I hugged the south side of the river, and as we entered a set of heavy rapids above the falls we cut diagonally towards the south shore portage trail through powerful, dark water.

Winston, Sloan and Victor were headed for the other side of the river. Winston and Tom handled the motors. Victor and I rode in the bows looking for boulders.

"Look out!" Victor screamed in a panic.

The bow of Winston's boat struck hard on a submerged boulder and lifted skyward, pointing straight up, and flipping backwards sending the men into the water.

Tom made a quick decision. Without thinking for his own safety, he gunned the engine and made his way across toward the three men. Winston, Sloan and Victor shouted for help and waved their arms as they bobbed up and down in the strong current carrying them towards the precipice.

"They are still reachable," Tom yelled at Charlie and me. The whitewater carried all of us toward the falls. Less than halfway across, our prop hit a boulder. We were thrown onto the bottom of the boat. The motor stopped. The river swung us to the far right side. We ricocheted from one boulder to another.

With the falls fast approaching, I curled up in a fetal position and wedged myself into the bow of the boat. Over we went. We were caught inside a washing machine. The stern of the boat went under and banged off of several rocks. The boat flipped over and threw us out against a solid granite outcropping. I hit the rock wall hard with my shoulder.

Still floating, but in terrible pain, the current whipped me around the

Moonshadows

point and shot me through a series of heavy rapids. I spotted Charlie. He was on his back, with his legs in front of him, going down the river.

I tried swimming, but the raging water controlled me. Only my life jacket kept me from going under. I spun around through the heavy current. The water was ice cold. Coughing and gasping for air, I struggled through what seemed endless rapids.

Kicking at the rocks, I saw Charlie again as he slammed into several sharp boulders, then disappeared into the even faster water near the shore.

The torrent flipped me and rolled me along the gravel bottom in the shallows. I tried to get to my feet, but the force of the current constantly knocked me down. I tumbled again, bouncing off some boulders and sliding over others. The water seemed to be gaining speed.

The river carried me until I spun into an eddy. I swam toward shore. My whole body ached. My swinging arms and legs hit the river bottom. The water was shallow, but it was hard to get up. My left shoulder hurt. Twice I tried to gain my feet; twice I fell to my knees.

I pushed hard with my right arm and got up. I looked around. Nothing could be seen. The rain came down in torrents and the sky darkened even more.

I started calling people's names, "Tom! Charlie!" I called out for several minutes, repeating their names. No answers came. I waded down the shoreline looking at the river for some hope. The Albany roared by me, a cauldron of whitewater. I waded further, still calling out, found one of the oars from the boat and threw it up onto the rocks.

"No one could be this far down," I thought. I couldn't comprehend the distance traveled during the disaster. I turned and walked the shallows upstream still calling out names, looking for the boat or anything I could find. Tom appeared around a point of land.

"Charlie! Mike!" Tom shouted, as he searched with his eyes across the noisy rapids.

"I'm here!" I shouted. "I'm here. Are you OK?" Tom saw me and we rushed toward each other in the shallow water.

"It's great to see you," Tom said, staring at me and shaking his head incredulously. His hair was hanging in his face and his heavy wet clothes were pasted to his body. "Are you OK?"

"Hell, I'm a survivor. Have you seen Charlie?"

"No. Where's Charlie?"

"I have no idea."

Tom seemed to have made it through the ordeal with no serious injuries. No visible signs of damage to his body.

I tried to rotate my left arm to see if it was all right, but the pain caused me to stop.

"What's wrong with your shoulder?"

"Banged it up a bit, but I think it's fine."

"I've got a few bruised ribs, but I don't think anything's broken," Tom replied.

"We came through this in pretty good shape. I thought we were going to die."

"I thought we were dead when we went over," Tom answered.

"Where do you think the rapids took the others?"

"I don't know," Tom said, "but just before we went over I saw Winston, Sloan and Victor go over the falls on the other side of the river."

"They're on the other side of the island?" I asked.

"Yes. I saw them," said Tom. He looked at me, then at the river.

"We've got to find the boat," he said. "Without a boat it will be hard to get back to camp. How do we rescue anybody? We need a boat."

Without a further word we started looking for Charlie. "Charlie," Tom said. "He's on this side. I hope he's all right." I nodded in agreement.

We waded the shallow water upstream, looking and yelling. A short time later we saw a body laying face up in a few inches of water near the shore. We ran towards him. I reached him first

Charlie coughed hard.

"Help me. He's alive!" I said as Tom approached.

Tom stood stunned for a moment and then went right to work, rolling Charlie over to help him expel the water from his lungs. Charlie started spitting up water. Tom stood him up. Charlie, still coughing, smiled at Tom and said, "Thanks," as he passed out.

"He'll be OK," Tom said. "Let's move him further up into the woods."

We dragged Charlie through 20 feet of shallow water and up a big piece of granite to a somewhat protected, wooded cove. We laid him against a large boulder under a tamarack tree.

We didn't know if the others survived. We were sure, however, that they were on the other side of the river. Tom and I were searching the river with our eyes when Charlie regained consciousness.

"What the hell happened?" Charlie said, coughing between words.

"What do you think happened?" Tom said.

"Good God," said Charlie, his beard drenched and speckled with debris. "What do we do now?"

"We survive," said Tom, trying to seem cool and calm. He had read at least a dozen books on survival and now it was his chance to use the information.

"Tom's right," I said. "We have to survive. There's nothing downstream for a hundred miles. We need to figure out a way to start a fire or we'll die from hypothermia."

I fumbled through my jacket and shirt pockets searching for my matches.

"Does anyone have any matches?" I asked. "Mine are gone."

Both Charlie and Tom are cigar smokers. They searched their pockets.

"I think I've got a lighter here somewhere," said Charlie. He rifled through his pockets, and then flipped his backpack over. Nothing fell out.

He lost everything in the rapids.

"Anyone have food?" Tom said.

"I've got two peanut butter and jelly sandwiches in zip-lock bags in my pack," I told him, "and two cans of Molson's."

"I've got the same," said Tom.

Although we had enough food for now, it would go fast. The cold, rain and dampness would quickly rob us of our energy. We needed to get dry soon, and we had no matches.

"There's only one thing to do," said Tom. "We've got to get back to the cabin." We began the walk back toward Grassi Lake where we would swim or build a raft to get across to our camp.

We made our own way down the treacherous shore, with no idea how far the whitewater had taken us. The situation all seemed like a dream, a terrible dream.

A driving rain fell from the darkening clouds so hard it hurt. The sky showed no sign of a break. The bitter cold storm only got worse. The temperature stayed just above the freezing mark.

I remembered one year when Victor and I were sitting in a boat on a sunny 60-degree day, and watched black clouds form on the horizon. We didn't think much about it, because the bad weather was North of us and the wind blew from the south.

Then the wind suddenly changed directions, sending the clouds quickly at us from the North and in 20 minutes a blizzard hit and the temperature dropped 25 degrees. An hour later it was over and there were three inches of snow in the boat. Then the wind shifted again, the sun came out and it warmed right up again.

The only way to tell weather in this area was to watch the sky. The climate could change within minutes. I prayed to God the sun would come out again.

The trek continued. We were stumbling along the rock-strewn shore when Charlie slipped on the wet granite, skidded downward across the surface and landed back in the river. He had cut his arm.

We waded in to help him get out of the frigid water. We started trembling.

"We must to do something now to stop the hypothermia," I said. "We're all shaking like hell."

"Let's eat now so we have some energy," said Tom.

We headed to the woods, sat down and each of us ate half a sandwich and drank a beer.

"It's not even noon and we're losing our coordination, and we still have a long way to go," I said.

Tom gave me a quick smile, "We'll get out of this. That cabin's going to feel pretty good."

Charlie didn't say anything. He sat on the ground huddled in his wet clothes and life jacket, dazed and shivering violently. After eating, we helped Charlie to his feet and continued up the shore. Charlie stumbled along and had trouble keeping the pace.

The woods offered no real shelter because we were already wet to the bone. A pall hung over us. We watched the water looking for a boat or debris from the tragedy. Everywhere looked dismal. Nothing existed to cheer us on.

Charlie started yelling the other men's names. "Winston! Sloan! Victor!"

"I told you they're on the other side." Tom said to Charlie.

"You don't know for sure," said Charlie. "They could be here."

"I saw the current take them," Tom insisted.

Charlie shook his head in disbelief.

Tom turned to me, "Between you and me, we walked over a mile of shore downstream before we found Charlie, and we have to be half way back to the base of the waterfall on our upstream hike together. We've covered a good two miles of river and haven't seen or heard from anyone. I say we keep going back to the cabin."

Tom's answer made sense.

"If they're on this side of the river we can't leave them here. They'd die before we came back to rescue them," said Charlie.

"That's irrational. No one is on this side," said Tom.

"I'm not going to go back and leave someone here to die," said Charlie.

"Charlie," Tom said. "Why are you forcing this issue? This is insane. There are boats, dry clothes and medical gear back at the cabin. We can get food for them. What can we do for them if we find them now? We're in pretty bad shape ourselves."

Charlie became enraged, "You selfish jerks," Charlie said facing us shivering. "I can't believe you guys. You want to leave them here."

"I don't want to leave anyone here. They aren't on this side of the island. We could kill ourselves looking for ghosts," said Tom.

"I'm staying!" Charlie said, shaking uncontrollably.

"I'm leaving," said Tom. "When I come back, I'll be ready to help. What are you ready to do?"

Caught between two friends, the decision was an easy one, almost too easy. "I'm going with Tom," I said.

"You selfish jerks," Charlie repeated.

"Come on," Tom said to me. "We don't have time to waste."

We turned together and started walking down the shore. After a hundred feet or so we glanced back. Charlie stood there trembling and glaring in our direction.

Tom continued with me toward the cabin and possible help.

Robert B. Gregg

Chapter 15

Winston swam to Victor as the falls approached. "Give me your arm," he called out to Victor. "Try to lay on your back!"

The current took them faster and faster. The river overpowered them. Winston extended his legs and kicked off a big rock. They churned over the waterfall. Victor hit a rock with his shoulder, knocking both of them towards shore.

Winston tried to swim, still holding tight to Victor's arm. "Stay with me," said the Cree. They kicked at the rocks together. Their life jackets kept their heads up, but they still swallowed water.

They were being battered constantly. A sharp boulder, just under the surface, violently knocked them apart.

"Stay up! Stay up," yelled Winston as they went their separate ways. Victor caught a glimpse of Sloan, and watched him disappear.

Winston tumbled along, backwards now, when he hit his head on a metal object, the blow spinning him around and depositing him in a shallow, gravel back-eddy. He struggled to gain his footing and as he stood, the swirling current knocked him down again. He swallowed more water.

Coughing from deep in his lungs, Winston regained his feet and searched the shore. It rained hard, and his whole body was in pain. Something sharp hit him in the back of the legs and he fell forward. He got up and reached back to push away the bow of his boat, floating upright and full of water. He grabbed the gunwale and struggled to pull it to a gravel beach.

Downstream, Victor struggled to stay alive. He tried to swim to shore, but the river controlled his every move. He tossed and turned and tumbled. Coughing, spitting, gagging, he fought the current.

"Just go with it," he thought. It wasn't as bad now. A strong, but easy flow carried him into a swirling pool, bumping him up against a flat, limestone outcropping. Victor tried to pull himself onto the ledge, but didn't have the strength. He hung onto the outcrop, suspended and rested.

"How wet can you get?" he thought. Victor gave his all, pulling himself up, and laid on the flat part of the rock shelf, staring up at the still darkening sky.

Something clutched him from the misty gloom. Startled, he turned his head.

"How are you doing buddy?" Sloan said smiling, looking like he had also gone through the rinse cycle, his right ear bleeding and dragging his left leg.

"I'm OK I guess. I'm tired and pretty beat up," Victor answered. "We're alive man. That's all that counts. How are you?"

"I need some help," Sloan said. "Something's wrong with my leg. I think the damn thing's broken."

Victor stood, reached down and hauled Sloan onto the shelf with both arms. Exhausted, they both sat down on the slick rock.

Sloan moved his hands down the side of his injured leg, felt a slight ridge and winced in pain.

"What's the diagnosis, doctor?"

"I've fractured my fibula."

"Bad?"

"Yes. I'm going to set the bone as best I can. I need your help. Find me a flat stick and tear off a piece of your jacket or shirt."

Victor found an eight-inch long, half-inch thick, split branch, and tore off the tail of his shirt.

"Will this do?"

"That should work."

Sloan sat up straight and moved his thumbs down his lower leg and set the bone in place. He screamed in pain when he did it.

"I've got the bone aligned. Now put the stick on the side of my leg where my thumbs are, and wrap it in place with the cloth before I pass out."

Victor followed his instructions, tightening the binding with a knot. "How bad is the break?" Victor asked.

"The fibula's not a weight-bearing bone. I'll be a crippled for a while, but I'll heal fine."

They sat back against the ledge wall to rest. The cold mist that accompanied the rain was lifting. Searching the river, Victor spotted Winston and the boat at the head of the pool. He yelled to Winston, "We're down here."

Winston stared into the storm, but did not see them at first. "Here on the ledge." Victor shouted.

"Try to come to me," called out the guide. "It's shallow and there's shelter in the woods."

"Can you swim?" Victor asked Sloan.

"I can make it. I'll just haul my bad leg."

They dragged themselves off the ledge and into the water. Swimming upstream together in the calm pool seemed easy after what they'd been through. A short way into their swim, Sloan screamed in pain as his broken leg hit the bottom, the water was shallow enough to walk.

Victor helped him up.

"Anyone hurt?" Winston asked.

"I'm not bad," said Victor, wading toward the boat, "but Sloan has a broken leg. We're tired, cold and beat up, but we're here."

They joined Winston on the beach. Their boat was nearby in a back eddy, upside down.

"Victor, help me roll the water out of this thing," said Winston. "Sloan, you sit on the beach and supervise."

They got on one side and heaved the 16-foot Lund straight up on its side. The water rushed out and returned to the river.

The boat was a bit beat up, but seaworthy. There was a ding just under the right bow and the engine cover was gone, but the motor seemed fine. The gas line was still connected and the clamps held. The gas tank survived.

"Will the engine start?" Victor asked.

"I hope so," said Winston.

They slid her back into the water. Winston got in and pulled the crank.

Nothing.

He cranked the motor several more times.

Nothing.

He adjusted the choke and the throttle on the handle.

He tried again.

Nothing. The engine didn't make a sound.

"Something's wrong," said Sloan.

"That's obvious," said Victor.

Winston looked at the engine. Suddenly, he reached down into the boat and squeezed the soft rubber bulb on the gas line. He pumped the bulb several times until it became hard as a rock. He pulled the crank. The engine sputtered and cut out. He opened the choke a little more, and yanked the cord again. The engine sputtered, coughed and spit out some strange bursts of smoke.

Winston closed the choke and the motor started to hum. They smiled a smile of relief. He waded to the head of the pool, and out further into the river.

"Now what?" Sloan asked.

Grey Wolf gazed upstream, studying the rapids. He motioned us closer to where he stood, and spoke, "Sloan, you get in the front and watch for rocks. Victor, sit in the middle and stay as centered as you can. I'm going to work my way up this shore, and when we get close to the falls I'm going to run the right side channel. I think the channel has enough water to clear the prop. If this works, we'll be back in a jiffy."

Victor helped Sloan climb aboard. Winston waded a little further out, holding onto the gunwale and keeping the craft pointed upstream. He slid over the side and into the back seat, grabbing the engine handle. They headed to the cabin.

Chapter 16

The weather became colder. The rain changed to sleet. The North wind blew harder where the river widened. Nothing but gloom faced us. The cold penetrated our wet clothes.

We walked, heads bowed down against the onslaught, for maybe half a mile. I followed Tom's lead.

We worried about Charlie. We knew he wouldn't survive alone. Charlie didn't respect the wild, and was not prepared for what lay ahead.

Charlie couldn't leave a friend behind. That's what we liked about him. He was a caring and thoughtful person, to a fault.

We slogged along, and then Tom stopped and faced me. "We've got to go back," Tom said, "He wouldn't leave us in this situation, and we're not going to leave him." Without answering I followed Tom and we trudged back together in the pouring rain.

"He can't survive without us," Tom said. "And, anyway, what would I tell my wife? That I just left her brother here to die?"

Charlie never took care of himself. He drank too much and smoked too much to endure the wild in a survival situation.

We both trembled as we walked the shore. "Sure would be nice if this rain stopped," said Tom, trying hard to change our thoughts.

"You bet," I answered. For some strange reason didn't seem worried. He was cool under fire and I thought, "We just went over a deadly waterfall and shot a few miles of wicked rapids and I'm still alive."

We heard Charlie before we spotted him. "Sloan! Victor! Winston!" he called out, and of course there was no reply.

A few steps later, we stood behind him.

"What are you doing?" Tom shouted, startling Charlie. "They're on the other side. Don't waste your energy."

Charlie cried. He stumbled over to us, and grabbed hold of Tom's arms.

"Now don't get mushy on me brother-in-law," said Tom. "We're still in a world of hurt."

"You're right," said Charlie. "The more I think about it, the more I know they're not on this side. I've wasted time, my time and now yours, I'm sorry."

"Don't worry about it. Let's get back to the cabin."

Our steamy breath could be seen when we talked. The heat was leaving our bodies. We needed to get dry. I kept trying to figure out a way to start a fire in these circumstances and came up with nothing. A college degree and 30 years of expeditions into the wild should have prepared me for this.

We walked together along the shore. The sky lightened up and we spotted the waterfall where the tragedy happened. It was a quarter mile upstream. I "flipped the bird" towards the cascading water in a fruitless gesture of anger.

Tom and I walked alongside one another. Charlie dragged behind, stumbling. We would stop and wait for him every few minutes. We hoped to arrive at the Grassi Lake portage before nightfall, but we still had 200 yards of granite wall and deep forest ahead.

"We've got to make faster time," Tom said.

Evening came fast and the rain seemed to be letting up. Past the hideous clouds clear weather was coming our way out of the Northwest.

"The weather is getting better," said Tom, pointing to the lighter sky along the horizon.

We were moving across a granite outcrop when Charlie fell, sliding steeply down towards the river into a tumble of jagged logs and large rocks. The biggest and sharpest log stopped him. Charlie shrieked in pain.

Tom and I sat down and cautiously slid to Charlie, lying on his back in the rocks and debris. He bled profusely from a gash that went deep into his leg, slashing him open to the bone.

I tore off the bottom part of my shirt and made a tourniquet.

Tom placed the tourniquet above the terrible wound and tightened gradually with a stick. We immobilized his leg and made him as comfortable as possible.

The bleeding continued. At the same time the rain stopped. Tom gently felt along Charlie's injured leg. "You've got one hell of a wound," he said.

Charlie tried to get up, but that only caused more bleeding.

"We've got to bandage that thing," I said.

Tom knelt down beside Charlie, took off his jacket, and made his undershirt into a makeshift bandage. I loosened the tourniquet. Charlie's pants were immediately saturated a dark red. Tom wrapped the leg tightly with the bandage. The bleeding slowed, but not enough. The huge wound wasn't clotting.

"We've got to get to the cabin," Charlie said bravely, trying to get up.

"Lay down. You're not going anywhere," said Tom, loosening the tourniquet. "You'll bleed to death if you keep moving. We need an alternate plan."

My brain went into overdrive. What the hell do we do now? Dozens of crazy plans, some logical, some not, came in and out of my thoughts.

The sun briefly burst through the clouds, but the temperature remained bitter cold. It would get colder yet when the sun went down.

"You're in the best shape," Tom said to me. "You must go to the cabin and get help. I'll stay here with Charlie and tend to his wound. I'm relying on you, Mike. Hell, we're both relying on you."

Charlie had fear in his eyes. He wanted to go, but he dare not move.

Confident I could make my way to camp, I stood ready to go.

"Before you leave," Tom asked, "could you help me get him up into the woods? We need some shelter."

Together we dragged Charlie up the slippery outcrop, losing our balance here and there, but staying on our feet. We found a dry spot in the forest and put him down.

Dark clouds were rushing above us. I still had a long way to go to get above the waterfall. I just hoped I'd have the strength to swim to the other side in the heavy current.

"I'll be back as soon as I possibly can," I said, and headed down to the rocky shore. I moved fast. Tom and Charlie needed me. The others needed me. I kept thinking of the cabin. Everything we needed was there; the medical supplies, and a boat and motor. Bound and determined, I jumped from rock to rock and waded across the shallow side channels.

Then I hit, what looked like, an insurmountable obstacle. The side channel in front of me was too deep to wade. I headed up, into the forest to go around the water. The woods were thick and the hiking tough. Deadfall was strewn everywhere. Trees crisscrossed like matchsticks in front of me. I tried to stay within sight of the river. I lacked a compass, and to get lost would mean not only my life, but also probably the lives of Tom and Charlie.

Robert B. Gregg

I climbed over the trees that had fallen at a waist high angle, and ducked under those trees that were higher. Sometimes I would climb up on a large one and walk the log like a tightrope to its end.

Following a brief but hellish battle with fallen trees and brush, I came to a huge wet ledge. Slippery and solid, the smooth rock extended at an angle towards the river. I slid down the face on my butt, and soon heard the roaring sound of the waterfall not far upstream.

I followed the shore as darkness took hold of the world. The going seemed easier, but my body was too tired to take advantage.

The wind now came out of the Northeast, and Northeast winds are not a good sign. It meant another storm was coming. A bitter cold overwhelmed me.

Following wolf tracks that went up the beach and into the woods, I found what I thought to be a path and continued along it for a while when the wind died down and I felt something hitting gently on my face.

It was snow, falling easily at first, simply drifting down. Then the storm hit and the wind gusted, driving the sharp flakes harder and harder.

"Please God, help me," I said out loud. My legs and hands tingled. I was trembling worse than ever.

Exhausted and hungry, I needed fuel. I decided to have the other half of my sandwich and the beer. I pulled the food from my pack as the snow surrounded me.

Unlocking the plastic bag, I took huge bites, and swallowed quickly. The peanut butter and jelly spread across the mushy bread tasted like filet mignon.

I struggled to open the beer. My frozen hands weren't working well. Finally, I concentrated all my power into the pop-top cap.

I heard the pleasant sound of the carbonation and never tasted a better beer.

After I ate, the going seemed easier, but that feeling didn't last. It became difficult to see. I repeatedly stumbled. The snow kept coming and the wind was lashing into a blizzard.

If I didn't have the river next to me, I wouldn't have known where I was. My brain wasn't functioning well. I became dizzy and I worried I'd pass out.

Moonshadows

I couldn't get rid of the cold. The chill stayed with me, penetrating my body. I never stopped shaking. My tingling fingers and hands ached in pain. The more I tried to keep from shaking the more I shook. I knew I was hypothermic.

I thought about sleep, but I wanted to keep moving. My mind was becoming unreliable. My body began to let me down. My feet weren't going where I pointed them. I meandered and stumbled like a buffoon. I needed shelter and had to get some sleep. I saw a hollow, large, fallen tree; I crawled inside and fell fast asleep.

Robert B. Gregg

Chapter 17

Winston steered the boat close to shore and worked his way towards the cabin and warmth. On the edge of fast water, he held steady, and cut right into a heavy current coming around a forested island. He followed the flow with caution until the channel turned left toward the lake.

"We're home free!" Victor shouted.

"Not yet!" Winston said.

As they rounded the bend, the bow was knocked sideways by a tremendous force of water coming out of the lake.

"Hang on," Winston yelled, gunning the engine to full power and regaining control. "It's going to be rough from here up into the lake."

They were pitched against a surge of water that was stronger than the whitewater rapids below the falls. The steep incline coming out of the lake was very forceful. There were no boulders to slow the current down. The river shot out of the lake in a smooth, swift slick.

Winston ran full throttle. They crawled inch by inch upstream. "Come on!" Winston urged the boat, struggling to make headway.

Sloan's face showed anxiety. Victor rocked forward and back, urging their boat onward. The trees along the bank slipped by at a snail's pace. Gradually they made the transition into the lake. They hugged the shore to avoid the current, gained speed and headed into the freezing rain.

"I'll go after the others after I get you guys back safe," said Winston, squinting as the sleet hit his face. "They could be injured, or dead for that matter, every second counts."

"We'll go with you," said Sloan.

"Yes," said Victor. "We're not leaving them out there."

"I'll go alone," said Winston emphatically. "I can handle the rapids better single-handedly and I'll have room to pick up three people and bring them back, "First, we have to get warm, put on dry clothes and gather clothes and gear for the others."

Arriving at the cabin, they beached the boat and raced inside. "Put some wood in the stove," Winston said to Victor. The coals were still hot and the dry logs blazed up immediately. They took off their wet clothes and put on dry. The cabin started to warm.

Sloan looked outside. "The weather is getting worse," Sloan shouted in anger. The others joined Sloan at the window. As they did, the winds picked up at a furious pace. The blizzard hit. The storm came from the northeast, from Hudson Bay. They couldn't see the lake.

Winston put dry clothes, warm jackets, three aluminum blankets and a first aid kit inside the emergency bag.

"Make me a pot of coffee. When you're done, fill a couple of thermoses," he directed Sloan. "Hand me that bag of cookies," he said to Victor.

As the coffee perked Winston explained what he would do. "They're on the other side," he said, putting on his waders and anorak. "I'll cross the lake and search below the falls. If I am not back by morning, one of you does the same. Do not try it together. The very survival of all of us may rest on someone being here when Ray comes in on the check flight. Understand?"

"We understand," said Sloan.

"Wish me luck gentlemen," Winston said as he grabbed a backpack loaded with coffee and cookies, the emergency bag, and went out into the night and the raging storm.

The door slammed shut.

Chapter 18

Tom and Charlie huddled together for warmth. Charlie's leg bled through the T-shirt bandage. Tom loosened the tourniquet to let blood get to Charlie's lower leg and foot for a bit and tightened it up again to keep him from bleeding to death. Charlie was getting weaker. His trembling was more intense, violent at times.

"Do you think Mike will make get back?" Charlie said in a feeble voice. His tired eyes pleaded with Tom for answers.

"If anyone can make it, Mike can," said Tom. "You stay close to me now and sleep." Charlie leaned on Tom and tried to sleep, but his shaking body wouldn't let him.

The wind whipped the snow against them. The night got quieter and colder. They huddled closer for warmth.

Charlie sensed life leaving him. He did not have the strength to fight any more. He shivered much more than Tom. Charlie sensed death taking him. "I can't feel my feet," Charlie said in panic. "Help me Tom. I'm going to die. I don't want to die."

"Hang in there, buddy. We just need to survive the night and we'll both be having hot coffee and Bailey's back at the cabin in the morning."

As each minute passed Charlie felt more numbness, his body ached. He contemplated death. He thought about his wife and what she was doing now. A beautiful woman, she was probably home now in a warm bed, reading a book.

He reflected on his daughter, his only child, beginning her first year of medical school.

What would they think of his death?

Tom fell asleep and dreamed of Key West. He was fishing offshore near an anchored shrimp boat and casting into a school of blackfin tuna From out of the dark blue sea a shadowy torpedo-like figure raced toward his bait. He readied himself for the coming strike when Charlie jolted him awake.

It was the middle of the night. Charlie was standing up. His wound was hemorrhaging, and Tom told him to sit down. Blood had turned his whole bandage bright red.

"I'm dying. Just leave me here. Save yourself. I have been a fool."

The temperature continued to fall and in the dark of early morning the stars broke through the clouds. The two men were covered in a light layer of snow.

"I'm sorry to be a burden." Tears streamed down Charlie's face. He shivered less. He seemed coherent.

"You're not a burden, Charlie. We're going to make it. Relax. Sit down."

Charlie's strength left him. He crumpled to the ground and curled up tight to Tom. He tried to convince himself that all would be OK. The river, the accident, the bitter cold, all distracted his thoughts from his family.

"I need to survive this," he thought. "If I could only get home I would be forever grateful. God, please let me see my family again."

Tom fell back to sleep. His shaking turned to a light trembling. His body reacted differently than Charlie's. Charlie wondered why. Charlie focused his thoughts on home. In his delirium and suffering, he saw his wife and daughter. They were sitting on the porch of his house in the sun.

Charlie was getting out of Tom's car, arriving back from the trip. He strolled up the walk and they rushed to him. They hugged him and kissed him. He put his arms around them. It was good to be home. He went to kiss his wife and then he awoke.

Surrounded by darkness, he coughed hard, the kind of cough that comes from deep in your lungs.

The sound jolted Tom awake from an intense sleep. "Take it easy, big guy," Tom said, holding onto Charlie.

Charlie quivered violently out of Tom's arms and collapsed face down in the snow.

Tom tried to lift him, but couldn't. He turned Charlie over. Then the strangest thing happened. Charlie pushed Tom down, and staggered to his feet.

"What are you doing?" Tom said.

"I'm dying," said Charlie as he began to rip off his clothes and drop them in front of Tom. "Let me die in dignity. I'm a dead man. Leave me here. It's OK."

"I'm not leaving you here. Sit down," Tom said rising to his feet. By the time he could reach him, Charlie had his vest and shirt off.

Tom faced Charlie in the night. Charlie reached out for him and fell, crumpling onto the ground. Tom knelt down to take Charlie's pulse.

Tom's hands quivered so bad he couldn't tell if Charlie was dead or alive. Then he looked at Charlie and realized there was no movement. No shivering, no nothing.

Charlie had passed on to a land where dreams do come true.

Tom lifted his body across his shoulders and started walking down the shore toward Grassi Lake.

He would not leave his friend to the wild.

Weak and weary, Tom's heart beat hard within his chest. He stumbled here and there, but plodded on. Step by step, he carried Charlie toward home.

He wanted to stop and sleep, but he fought the feeling. He became dizzy. The snow began to lighten up and dawn would be breaking soon. Tom continued his quest for the lake.

Hope lay ahead.

Robert B. Gregg

Chapter 19

The snow raged around him, and gathered inside the boat.
"They must be suffering," Winston thought.
He hugged the tree-lined shore to stay out of the wind, but when he ventured out to cross the lake, the driving snow forced him to keep his head down. Here and there he looked up as he motored across and downstream toward the portage at the treacherous falls.
The rescue had to go well. Three lives hung in the balance.

Winston felt some trepidation as he approached the rapids above the falls. He steered with his left hand while shining his flashlight at the shore ahead. The beam of light glared off the blowing snow. Visibility was less than poor. He could not see far. He moved cautiously and slow.
He stayed along the shore to avoid the fast current and big rocks. This time he wanted more control. The storm let up a little. He had no one in the bow to look for obstacles, but he felt safe. He read the water better than any white man.
Winston knew the river. He guided on it for over 20 years. His only fault came in trusting his client's judgment too much and now disaster had struck, and he had allowed it to happen.
Winston was determined to rescue them. He prayed to God they were all right. "It's hard to kill a man, Lord," he said out loud. "Please keep them alive until I reach them."

Moving along the shore, Winston used his flashlight to search for the opening to the portage. He spotted the yellow ribbon that marked the path ahead. He tied up the boat and followed the trail to the high point above the falls, climbed up but the visibility was zero. The high point offered no advantage.
The wind blew hard down the river. He felt the stinging snow on his face. Winston decided to search on foot. He hiked down to the wooded shoreline trail and searched amongst the strewn trees for almost an hour and found nothing. He cried out their names many times, but heard no reply.
Winston confronted the reality that the flashlight simply glared off the falling snow, providing him with little vision, and the sound of the

howling wind and the river wiped out his voice. Exhausted, he would be no help now even if he found them. He decided to return to the cabin.

He called out one last time. "Tom! Charlie! Michael!"

No answer came.

The snow showed no signs of stopping. He turned and followed the portage path back to the boat.

His eyes searched as much as possible, but he found no sign of the men.

Arriving at the boat, he untied it and made the perilous journey across the dark waters of the lake back to the cabin.

Morning was sure to bring better conditions. Tomorrow had to be a better day.

Chapter 20

They sat in the gloom of the cabin. The lantern cast eerie shadows across the interior. They thought about their friends in a blizzard in the dead of night.

"I can't believe we let Winston cross the lake alone. If anything happens to him what will we do?" Victor said.

"He knows what he's doing," said Sloan.

"Are you crazy? Didn't you hear about him running those wild rapids in front of Charlie and Mike?"

"This is different. He won't take any chances tonight. He's not going to perish in the black of night with people's lives on the line."

"I guess you're right."

The wind howled outside. The situation did not bode well for the others.

"Do you think they're all right?" Victor asked.

"Yes. They can take care of themselves. Tom will keep them safe."

"Don't worry, Victor, if anybody is able to find them in this storm, it's Winston."

Sloan limped over and stoked the woodstove. He peered out the window. The light from the cabin shone off the snow that was still coming down, but beyond that existed nothing but blackness, deep blackness. He went back to the table and sat.

The men remained there fidgeting with books and magazines, reading a little, and then staring at the walls. They were nervous, not for themselves, but for their companions somewhere in a frigid hell, fighting for their lives.

"How long do we wait?" Victor said.

"Until we can wait no longer," said Sloan.

Dark thoughts played in their minds.

"Are the other men hurt? How badly were they hurt?"

The more they tried to drive out these depressing thoughts, the worse the thoughts became.

"Were they dead? How many were dead?"

Victor laid his head down on his arms and went to sleep. Soon, the warmth of the cabin and the exhaustion of the day caught up with Sloan.

He rose from the bench and crawled inside his sleeping bag and his thoughts vanished with his consciousness.

Moonshadows

Chapter 21

Grey Wolf returned to the cabin. He came through the door, his head down, wearing the backpack and dragging the emergency bag. Dejected and exhausted, he slumped into a chair.

"Where are the others?" Sloan said from his bag.

"I could not find them."

Victor woke and rubbed his eyes and the back of his neck.

"Did you reach the portage?" Sloan inquired.

"Yes. And I walked the bank of the river below the falls."

"Did you find anything?" Victor asked.

"Nothing. I will try again early in the morning. Hopefully, the storm will clear. For now, we all need to rest."

Victor got up and paced the cabin as Winston took off his gear and crawled into his sleeping bag.

"Get some sleep," the guide said. "And set the alarm for six."

"What if it is still blowing and snowing?" Sloan said from the comfort of his bunk.

"The weather doesn't matter," said Winston. "Tomorrow morning, no matter what, I have to go."

Victor set the alarm clock, turned off the lantern and got in his bag. The cabin became silent, but they listened, as the wind gusted and howled outside, and thought about their friends.

The alarm rang loudly.

"What the hell is that?" Sloan yelled, and soon remembered the situation.

The rising sun lit the cabin.

Winston jumped out of his bunk and hurried outside to check the weather. It had warmed. The snow was quickly melting. A blue sky greeted him, extending from horizon to horizon. He came back inside, stoked the woodstove and reheated the coffee he had poured out of the thermoses and into a pot.

"God has given us a miracle," he said to Victor and Sloan. "I've got to get going. Every minute counts." His energy amazed them.

Victor and Sloan got up, the coffee was hot, and by the time they filled the thermoses Winston was ready to go. They walked outside together.

"Let us hope God has also been kind to the others," Winston said, getting into the boat. He re-filled the gas tank, and waved goodbye.

Winston followed the route he took the night before and soon found himself at the portage. Arriving, he hauled the boat over the short trail to the back eddy below the falls and launched into the rapids.

He stayed close to shore, avoiding the rocks and debris, motoring downstream. Searching the woods and the banks, Winston looked for anything that would give him proof the others were alive.

He watched the shore with hope in his heart. Exploring for movement, for tracks in the snow, anything that would lead him to the others. He went around a granite outcrop and saw a beam of sunlight hitting a piece of bright yellow cloth near the base of a tree.

Chapter 22

I dreamed I heard the sound of the boat motor getting louder and louder. I awakened inside the tree hollow, rigid, like a corpse. I tried to get up to signal, but I didn't have the strength. I was light-headed and my muscles wouldn't work.

The sound of the motor became more pronounced. A voice called from the river. At first I failed to understand the words and then they came loud and clear.

"Mike! Mike!" a voice cried out.

Sunbeams streamed through the snow-covered branches of the tree. I looked at the shore, glistening under a beautiful blue sky. Forcing myself up on my hands and knees, I crawled outside as a boat approached the land in front of me.

"Mike, are you alright?"

I gathered all the power left in me to answer but mumbled something incoherent and not loud enough for him to hear.

"Where are Tom and Charlie?" Winston yelled, beaching the boat.

"They're downstream," I said, trying to stand, but falling on my knees.

Winston raced up the shore with a bag slung over his shoulder. He helped me up. I shivered violently, and then it would stop, and start up again. My body remained out of control. "I can't stop shaking," I said apologetically.

"Don't worry," said Winston. "You'll be fine soon."

I kept thanking him as he exchanged my wet clothes for dry.

Winston helped me down to the boat and gave me cookies and hot coffee. He put a fleece blanket around my shoulders.

The sun rose in the sky. It warmed me like bread in a toaster.

"Thank God, I got to you just in time," Winston said. "You look near dead. You must have spent quite a night."

"I don't know," I said. "I don't remember."

"You are fortunate," said Winston. "If you hadn't found that hollow tree trunk you might have frozen to death." Winston smiled and added, "But I think you're going to make it."

"Where is everybody else?" I asked.

"Victor and Sloan are back at the cabin. They're beat up pretty bad,

Robert B. Gregg

but they'll be OK.

"We thought you had all drowned," said Winston. "We got back to the cabin at about eight last night. I changed into dry clothes, grabbed some rescue gear and came almost this far last night, but even with flashlights, the snow and wind made my search impossible. I decided to regroup and try again early this morning."

The urgency of the current situation hit me. "We have to get Tom and Charlie," I said. "When I left them, Charlie's leg was badly injured and he couldn't walk. Tom stayed with him to help. They're downstream."

"We'll go as soon as you're ready," said Winston.

"I'm ready now," I said, still quivering.

Winston helped me into the boat and we worked our way down through the rapids, sticking close to shore so we could spot them in the woods.

The sun, along with the dry wool socks and boots, long poly underwear, and down jacket, slowly brought my body back to life. I shoved oatmeal-raisin cookies in my mouth and drank the warm coffee. I sat in the bow facing Winston, turning every once in a while to search the shore.

"Do you remember where you left them?" Winston said.

"Not exactly," I said. "I hope I can recall the spot." We rounded a bend in the river and observed Tom laying face down in the snow.

"My God," Winston said as he slid the boat ashore.

Winston rushed to Tom, still alive, but breathing in small gasps. He turned him over and noticed Charlie's torn and bloody pants in his hands. Winston carried him back to the boat and we started putting dry clothes on him. Tom regained consciousness. I gave him some cookies and coffee.

"What happened to Charlie?" I asked.

"Charlie's dead," Tom said. "What am I going to say to my sister? Charlie's dead. There was nothing I could do. I carried him..." His voice trailed off and his teary, wide eyes showed tragedy and loss.

Winston grabbed the coffee and cookies just before Tom fumbled them. Tom passed out into a deep sleep.

"He'll be all right," said Winston.

He stayed unconscious while we finished dressing him and wrapped him in an aluminum blanket. We made him as comfortable as possible on the several dry life jackets in the bottom of the boat.

We proceeded down river in the hope Charlie had survived. A little ways down, Winston got out and picked up a paddle lost the day before. We continued our search. About a quarter-mile further we spotted Charlie lying like a rag doll in the snow. He wore only his bloodied long johns, shoes and socks.

Winston got out and walked over to him. He checked his pulse. Nothing. "He's dead," Winston said, still holding his fingers on the artery in Charlie's neck.

"Make sure," I said to Winston. "Sometimes hypothermia victims will have no noticeable pulse and can still be alive." I prayed Charlie endured with us.

Winston held the first three fingers of his right hand on Charlie's throat. He felt nothing but the cold.

"What now Mike?" Winston said to me.

"Do you know CPR?"

"Yes."

"Do it," I said.

Chest compressions and breathing warm air into Charlie's cold lungs brought no response.

Winston rose from Charlie's corpse and looked up the beach. It was a sight he will never forget.

"Look," he said to me, pointing up the shore. I sat up higher in the boat and gazed down the bank of the river.

As far as the eye could see, there were only Tom's footprints in the snow. He had carried Charlie's body down the entire shore before dropping it and staggering on to where we found him.

Winston lifted Charlie's body, cradled it, and carried him back to the boat and laid it down gently.

I slumped back down into the seat. Tom awoke and reached for Charlie's body.

"He got so cold last night," Tom said, hugging Charlie around the neck. "Then he got quiet. I held him in my arms. He died in my arms." Tom cried as he stared into Charlie's faded, empty face.

"If Charlie hadn't left the emergency bag on the dock; if he wore better shoes, if he had on hiking boots instead of sneakers, if he weren't so clumsy, he would probably be alive. I should have taken better care of him."

"Don't blame yourself," Winston said. "The river killed him, not you."

Indians attribute almost all occurrences in life to nature and spirits. Maybe they're right.

Winston gave both of us more coffee and we sat hugging the cups and sending the warmth into our bodies.

"You guys have been through hell," Winston said.

"What happened to the others?" Tom said. It was typical of Tom to think first of other people.

Winston told him about Victor and Sloan.

"You were a lot more fortunate than us," Tom said and turning to me asked, "And where did Winston find you?"

"A mile upriver," I said. "I crawled in an old tree hollow to die, but Winston decided to rescue me instead."

"What happened to Charlie's clothes?" Winston asked Tom. (I had wanted to ask the same question.)

Tom started to cry again, and then regained his composure. "Charlie acted crazy toward the middle of night," Tom said. "He stood up, and I told him to sit down, because his wound was hemorrhaging. He kept telling me he was dying and that I should just leave him. I said I wasn't going anywhere."

Tom told us Charlie began taking off his clothes and giving them to Tom.

"You need them more than me," Charlie told Tom.

"I tried to put them back on him and he wouldn't let me," Tom said. "Then he quivered violently and collapsed. I think that's when he died. I don't know."

Tom said he didn't want to leave Charlie's body out in the wilderness for the wolves so he carried him down the shore hoping to get help.

"I had to do something. I had to at least bring his body back."

Winston pushed the boat off and we motored up to the last upstream portage below the dreaded falls. The three of us dragged the boat with Charlie's body up and over the portage into Grassi Lake.

We headed for the cabin in silence.

Chapter 23

As we approached the shore, Victor came out and down to the boat. Sloan followed him using an old oar as a crutch. Winston pulled alongside the dock. I sat in the middle, wrapped in a blanket, more tired than I have ever been. Tom, holding Charlie's body in his arms, carried a sad melancholy in his eyes.

"I'm sorry about Charlie," said Victor to Tom.

"Thanks," he replied.

"Nice to see you moving around," Winston said to Sloan.

"I'm feeling better."

Winston got out and secured the boat. Victor reached out and helped me out, then held out his hand for Tom, but Tom just sat in the boat holding Charlie. Tom stared straight ahead as if in a trance.

"Come on now, Tom," said Winston. "Grab hold of Victor's hand. We will take care of Charlie."

Tom reached up and Victor helped him out. Winston and Victor removed Charlie's body and carried it up to the cabin. They put him down inside the screened-in porch.

Charlie lay on his back, his pale, dead eyes gazing up at the rafters. His jaw hung loose.

"What now?" I asked Tom.

"I don't know," he said. "This is something you don't plan for."

We went inside and gathered at the table. Victor offered a glass of Scotch to everyone. Winston didn't drink.

"Mike," said Winston. "Do me a favor and grab Charlie's sleeping bag." I got up and gathered Charlie's bag into my arms.

"I need a couple of guys out on the porch," said Winston.

Without a word being spoken, we all stood up and walked back to the screened-in porch. Tom proceeded to take the rest of Charlie's bloodied clothes off him.

Victor unzipped the bag all the way down. Winston and I slid Charlie's naked, dead body into the bag, and Tom zipped it up, gazing a moment at his pale and cold lifeless face, as if to say his last goodbye, and made the sign of the cross.

"Rest in peace, buddy," he said.

We went back in the cabin. There was a pall in the room.

"We survived," said Tom to me. "I guess you could say we're lucky, but Charlie's dead."

"I'm going to get some lunch going," I said.

"Sounds good," said a recovering Sloan.

Sloan was a disaster. There was a big welt on his forehead, his right ear was cut horribly and he walked like every bone in his body was bruised or broken.

"Sit down, Sloan," I said. "I hurt just watching you."

"We need help," Tom said. "And we need it now. We've got to stay calm and think this situation out."

Victor came back in and we all sat at the table and listened to Tom.

"I'll ask the guys in the cabin across the lake to fly me and Charlie's body back to Nakina. I'll call my sister and take care of what has to be done. I'll hire a plane to take me home. There's no sense ruining your vacation."

"You fly the body out and send a plane back," said Sloan. "We are all leaving together."

Chapter 24

We took two boats across the lake to the other cabin to ask for help, Tom and I in the lead boat, Winston and Victor in our wake. Sloan stayed at camp.

The high water was hard to traverse and the powerful river current swept down the middle of the lake often carrying large uprooted trees.

We started by going upstream, in order to calculate ending up in front of our destination.

"Getting them to help shouldn't be a problem," I said to Tom.

"I don't think so," said Tom. "The flight will only take a few hours of their time."

The traverse took longer than expected. The surging river got stronger as we neared the main current and, combined with a heavy crosswind, made the short trip an expedition.

"Now I have an idea of what kind of hell those guys went through yesterday," said Tom.

"Sloan told me they took almost an hour to work up the side channel and around the falls," I said.

I turned toward the front to search for debris when I perceived a branch out of the corner of my eye. "Look out!" I yelled. Tom took a quick turn to port and we escaped disaster. An immense tree limb swept past our boat. We dodged several more enormous pieces of timber before approaching the shore.

As we neared the riverbank, four fishermen came out of the cabin. One carried a rifle. All four had holstered handguns. Tom nosed our boat up into the mud. Winston and Victor pulled up on our left.

"Welcome," said a tall man with chiseled features and a square chin. "What can we do for you?"

"We need your help," said Tom. "One of our party has been killed in a terrible accident and I wondered if you would be kind enough to fly me and the body back to Nakina?"

"The will of," said another man before the lanky stranger who gazed at us with piercing blues eyes cut him off.

"We are sorry you have lost your friend," he said, "but we cannot fly you anywhere."

We were surprised.

"Is not your outfitter's plane coming in a few days to check on you?" another added. "You can fish until then."

His statement was so cold and heartless we found the words hard to believe.

"Are you kidding me," said a stunned Tom? "What the hell is wrong with you?"

"Didn't you hear me," said the stranger. "I will not argue."

Flustered, Tom hesitated and tried to calm down.

"We will pay you, if that's the problem," he said, begging for understanding.

"This is not a matter of money."

"If not a matter of money, then what?"

The man did not answer, but turned and started walking back to the cabin. Tom questioned the other men.

"Can any of you fly the plane besides him?"

"No," said a young man in his early 30's with a day's worth of whiskers on his face. "Do not push this. Go back to your camp."

"You're our only hope," said Tom in desperation.

"We can't wait until the check flight arrives," Winston yelled, sitting in the stern of his boat. "When you are in need in the bush you help one another. This is the Law of the North."

None of them answered.

Victor got out of the boat and walked over to the other strangers. The other two men just stood and stared at us.

"Come on man. Talk to the guy."

"Leave now," said the frightening one, with the red headband, who seemed constantly angry, and had been quiet up to this point.

The tall man stopped short of the cabin door and turned to confront us. His face was twisted in rage and he screamed at the others. "We cannot let them go."

"You're right," said the angry one, and pointed his rifle at Tom and me.

"Don't move," he said. The other man drew his pistol and aimed at Victor.

"What the hell," said Victor.

"Get over by your friends," the man said.

Moonshadows

At that moment, Winston cranked the engine, threw the motor into reverse, and plowed backwards, water surging over the stern.

As Winston turned the boat, the man with the headband raised his rifle, aimed, and fired.

The bullet hit Winston above his eyes. Blood poured out of his head and his body toppled into the lake. The boat, engine still running, made small circles and was taken away by the current.

Victor became indignant. He faced the shooter. "Why?" he fumed. "Why did you shoot him?"

The man turned and pointed the rifle at Victor, leveling the barrel close to his face. "Shut your mouth, you infidel," he said.

"Don't shoot," Tom yelled at the man.

"Easy, Victor," I cried out. "Easy."

Victor froze, his face full of rage and contempt.

"Don't be a fool," the tall man said to Victor. "Trying to be a hero will just leave you dead like your Indian friend."

We were captured. One thing we knew for sure. They were cruel and quick to anger.

"Tie them up inside," the tall man told the others, his eyes filled with rage.

"Why have you killed the Indian? He was an innocent man. It is forbidden to attack noncombatants," the younger one said to the shooter. "Ahmad, the soul of man is sacred and an attack on him is an attack on all humanity."

"You should have never come, Joseph," said Ahmad. "You are soft and should have been left with the women."

"The Prophet has said, 'Whoever slays a soul, it is as though he slew all men,'" said the younger man.

"Now you quote me the Koran," said an angry and grim Ahmad. The Koran also says, 'And one who attacks you, attack him in like manner as he attacked you,' and also, 'Fight for the sake of Allah against those who fight against you.'"

"Enough. Enough," said the tall leader to the men. "Ahmad, Abraham take them into the cabin and tie them tightly, and you, Joseph, bring me some tea."

"Yes, Fouad," said Joseph, the younger man.
Fouad? Ahmad? Abrahim? Who were these men?
There was only one possible answer.

Chapter 25

Tom and I are tied to chairs with duct tape. Victor is bound and sitting on the floor between the chairs. The tape that secured us cut into our wrists and ankles. We weren't going anywhere.

The cabin interior is identical to ours, right down to the picnic table and wood-burning stove.

The leader approached us.

"My name is Fouad Habib. My brother here is Joseph. These men are Ahmad and Abraham. That is all you need to know."

"Are you terrorists?" Tom asked.

"You are the terrorists," said Fouad, calm and determined. "And you must die."

"We have done nothing to you," said Victor. "Why are you doing this? This is against the teachings of the Koran?"

"Beware of their words, my brother," Fouad said to Joseph. "They are just trying to save themselves. They will die like the liars and deceivers they are."

Ahmad kept the sinister grin forever frozen on his face. Abraham came over and stood in front of us. He was also a frightful man with dirty teeth and a lame leg. He wore an old headband of red that kept his long black hair in a semblance of control.

"Their words are but false and futile lies. The Americans support Israel's aggression against the Palestinian people and occupy Arab lands and steal our oil," Ahmad said.

Fouad didn't look like an evil man. He smiled pleasantly at times and would grin sometimes at whatever anyone said, even if it wasn't humorous. He was a hard read. He walked over to Ahmad and shouted in his face. "You talk too much, and your talk has condemned them."

"Condemned them," I thought. The realization of our impending death sent fear through my body. I glanced at Tom and Victor in terror.

"Where is the other man," said Fouad.

"Why should we tell you?" Victor said.

"Because if you do not, we will kill you, one by one," said Fouad, placing his gun against Victor's forehead. "This is not a game. Tell me where he is."

117

"Never," Victor said, looking up at Fouad's face.

A loud bang exploded and Victor toppled over backwards. His blue eyes were still open, looking lifelessly at me, a small hole centered in his brow. Very little blood came out of the hole. The back of his head was shattered, and blood poured out, forming a pool of crimson on the floor.

"Tell me now where he is or I will kill your friend," Fouad directed Tom, while shoving the gun barrel against my ear.

"He's back at the cabin," Tom hurriedly said, "but there's no reason to shoot us."

"What is his name?"

"Sloan," said Tom. "He's a doctor and a good man with a family. You have no justification to kill him or any of us. We mean you no harm."

"Go across and find this Dr. Sloan and kill him," said Fouad to Abraham and Ahmad. "And take this infidel's body out of here and throw it in the river."

Chapter 26

Using his binoculars, Sloan observed his friends' boat motor across the river and beach on the far shore.

Four men came out of the cabin. "They're armed," he thought. "Why are they armed?" The men had an argument. He noticed Tom pleading with them.

One man pointed a rifle at Victor, Tom and Mike. Winston gunned his boat backwards, they shot him and he fell into the lake.

"They've killed him," said Sloan to himself. "Why?"

Sloan watched them argue. Then Tom, Mike and Victor were taken into the cabin at gunpoint. Later, he heard a shot. Shortly after, two men dragged Victor's body out of the cabin and down to the lake where they threw it into the shallows. The two men got into one of the boats and started across. They were coming for him.

"They've killed Winston and Victor. The trapper's cabin!" he thought. "I must get to the trapper's cabin. I'll have shelter, and a gun."

The crossing would take the strangers several minutes because of the heavy current. Sloan rolled up his sleeping bag, and filled his backpack with energy bars, bread, peanut butter, jam and four bottles of beer. On the way out of the door, he remembered the bear spray, went back in and snatched the can off the shelf.

He left the cabin going to the east, hoping that if they saw him, they would go that way. He promptly doubled back to the west, to the trail to the trapper's cabin.

In their rush across the lake, the men did not see where Sloan went.

Sloan stopped at the outhouse, went in, took a roll of toilet paper, shoved it in his pack and climbed through the heavy growth to pick up the trail to the trapper's cabin. "There's no sense moving the camouflage debris at the opening and putting it back," he thought. "I'll just go around it."

The load was heavy, but Sloan moved down the trail like a man on a mission. Limping on his makeshift crutch, he zigzagged through the dense woods. In his haste, he stumbled and fell several times, each fall more painful than the last.

By the time he reached the refuge of the cabin his muscles ached, and he collapsed, exhausted, onto the cabin floor, leaving the door open behind him.

He was alone, really alone. His friends were dead or captured. As long as he could hear the noise from the boat engine, he was safe.

After a quick break, he stood and surveyed the shelter. In the corner he saw the shotgun. He went over, loaded the chamber with slugs, and put some extra shells in his pockets. He felt more secure now. He could defend himself.

A plan. He thought about a plan.

The sound of the boat motor stopped. The strangers were at their cabin. Discovering him gone, they would surely continue their search.

He couldn't take the chance. He took the gun and his gear and left, heading west along the bluff, always keeping the lake in view.

This would be a bad time to get lost.

Sloan moved almost unconsciously, like an animal. He was confident. The sweat of his effort pasted his dark blond hair against his scalp. He crouched down so he wouldn't be seen. His life and the lives of the others depended on his survival.

The wilderness of beauty and peace that he loved had become a dark, brooding hell of the most dangerous game. 'To kill or be killed' turned out to be reality.

Sunset came swiftly. With less light, Sloan became even more aware of his surroundings. He no longer bumped into things or stumbled. He adapted to the wilderness and his balance seemed to suddenly improve.

Sloan liked this cat and mouse game with the murderous strangers. He was an intelligent man and intelligent men usually win. He would never give up hope. He was stronger than that.

Sloan did, however, have his weakness, his fear of the dark. He drove the thought from his mind. It was not a pleasant one anyway. Sloan remained anxious, with good reason.

He heard the boat motor again. The strangers were going downstream from the camp in the opposite direction. Sloan waited, kneeling in the brush a quarter mile upstream from his refuge.

About an hour later the strangers came his way along the shore, gazing into the forest for any sign of their lone adversary. They seemed relentless in their pursuit.

Cruising right by where the trapper's cabin stood, they passed Sloan and noticed nothing. Coming back downstream, they followed the shore again looking for him.

"They don't know where I am." Sloan thought, as he followed them with the binoculars.

As they looked for him, he became the watcher. They motored by again. Just short of the upstream rapids, they crossed the lake and sped back to their cabin.

They had given up, for now.

He returned to the safety of the trapper's cabin.

Robert B. Gregg

Chapter 27

"Why do we kill? It is written, we cannot kill unless in self-defense," Joseph said to his brother. "These men have not attacked us. We have no quarrel with them."

"They are Christians and you are talking foolishly, my brother."

"We cannot stop you. Why kill us?" Tom asked.

"We will kill you, because we cannot allow anyone knowing how we did this," said Fouad.

"Nothing can stop us now," said an arrogant Fouad with a sinister voice. "Your President is giving a speech in Ottawa tomorrow about how he will bring destruction to ISIL. We will proceed, as you say, to crash the party."

Fouad's face consisted of deep, dark eyes and an ample brow. He paced constantly and was high-strung and easily irritated.

"The plane will serve us well," he said with an evil grin. "We will fly below any radar, to our destination. We need not stop, because we have rigged one of the gas drums to feed our fuel tank, if necessary." He spoke almost casually of his plan for assassination and suicide.

What made him a radical? Why do radical Muslims get inspired to kill innocents, even their own people?

"Why do you hate these men?" Joseph asked his brother.

"I have personally seen their exploitation," said Fouad. "The alcohol, the womanizing, the drugs. The Arab world is tainted by its relationship with the West. The corruption is beyond belief. While many citizens are poor, our sheiks sit in their palaces watching your evil movies, drinking alcohol, and crapping in gold-plated bathrooms. I will no longer tolerate this influence of the West."

He turned away from us and ran his fingers over the Koran on the table. "We practice the purified faith. The faith passed down from the Prophet Mohammed."

He walked over to us.

"We are Sunni Muslims," he said, getting so close to my face his foul breath forced me to turn away. "We are the pure, untainted ones. We are followers of the ninth-century scholar Ahmed ibn Hanbal. He was a great man who urged his followers to abide by the Koran and the Sunna, the gospel of Mohammed himself. We Sunni keep strictly to the Koran. We are against anything Western. We keep women in their place."

The men who held us were fanatics. Their expressions showed the rage they held within.

"We put the Saudi royal family in power over 200 years ago, and we will take them out of power if they do not come to their senses."

Fouad walked away and sat down at the table. He studied a detailed map of the Parliament Building in downtown Ottawa. All remained quiet for a while.

The brothers sat, drinking their tea and occasionally looking out the window.

"I was once a student at Harvard," Fouad said, breaking the silence. "I could not stand the place. It is the home of falsehood. Of people saying one thing and meaning another."

He got close to Tom's face this time. I think he was trying to intimidate and toy with us.

"The Americans said they would help us defeat the Russians in Afghanistan, and as soon as the war ended, they took over. We Sunnis are intolerant toward false forms of Islam. The Muslims of Iran are Shi'a. I hate the Iranians. They do not follow the Koran as true believers," he said. "We are establishing the worldwide caliphate. And we will kill millions to establish our reign. I should shoot you now just because I despise you. Consider yourselves fortunate."

His hostility was amazing.

The two returned from their search for Sloan and entered the cabin.

"Well, what is your report?" Fouad asked.

"We have seen no signs of this other man, this Sloan," responded Abrahim.

"This Sloan is a danger to us," said Ahmad. "We should kill these two infidel pigs now and be done with them."

"Leave these men to me. I keep them alive because they humor me," said Fouad with an evil smirk. "No killing for now. They are good bait for this Sloan."

"I would kill them," said Ahmad before leaving the cabin. He walked out, slamming the door in defiance.

The leader laughed, turned to us and said, "Ahmad is young and impatient, but he is willing to die for our cause. I also am willing to die. Are you willing to die for anything?"

We did not answer. His arrogance and contempt for us was obvious. His hate overwhelmed him. What could we say to halt his tirade? When we were captured the light of day shone through the windows. Now the shadows lengthened. The woods were turning dark.

Fouad appeared ready to die. My only thoughts were about surviving this madman's wrath.

He stared out the window toward the lake. The silence didn't last long. "We are ISIL," he said, turning to face us. "We are prepared to serve our leaders when they need us. Today they need us to kill and we will kill. I want you to know this before you die."

"What is the purpose of this hatred? Your leaders are out for their own gain. They're not putting their life on the line. Don't you see that?" I added.

"Let us kill them now," Abrahim interrupted.

"I told you I need them for bait," Fouad said. "We need to eliminate their friend. This Sloan will come back to rescue them. Then we will kill them, each and every one, and get out of here."

"Why should he come back? What if he is a coward and just hides in the woods?" Abrahim said.

"They are his friends. This Sloan will come to us," Fouad answered.

Fouad sat in deep thought, and turning he said to Abrahim, "Tell Ahmad to search the shore again. Let's keep pressure on this Sloan."

Abrahim went outside.

"Ahmad, make another run to look for this Sloan."

"Gladly," answered Ahmad. He loaded a rifle into the boat and smiled at Abrahim.

"I'll bring you back his body."

He headed across the lake to kill Sloan.

Robert B. Gregg

Chapter 28

Our annual fishing trip had become a horrible and deadly ordeal.

Sloan appeared unnerved, but ready. The mad dash through the woods put a lot of pressure on his broken leg, and it throbbed in excruciating pain. He popped several painkillers and slugged down part of a beer.

The call of the loons, once elegant and magical, awakened his senses and shot fear through him. He constantly glanced about nervously. As a boy, he was always afraid when the lights went out. His time in an Iraqi dungeon made his problem worse. Sloan hid those fears all his life, but fought them.

"There are scary things in the gloom of night," he said to himself, repeating Winston's words. Now his fears of the dark overwhelmed him.

"I am becoming paranoid," he reasoned.

"But even paranoids have enemies," he laughed out loud at the thought.

Laying the gun on the floor, he pulled himself inside his sleeping bag. Tired and cold, the bag warmed him. He began to get drowsy. Exhausted, he fell fast asleep. Not long after, a wolf howled and he woke, and crawled out of the bag.

"Don't get too comfortable, Sloan," he said to himself. "Get too comfortable and you're dead."

He sat with his back against the wall, and hunger took hold of him. He hadn't eaten since breakfast. Opening his backpack, he removed some cookies and sat on the floor eating, and drinking a beer, intently listening to the sounds outside.

When he finished, he got up and went outside. The night sky was clear, with a few small clouds drifting by. The cold air made him shiver.

A pale white moon climbed behind him to meet the stars.

Sloan stood the shotgun against a tree and knelt behind some thick bushes. Putting his binoculars to his eyes, he zeroed in on the cabin across the lake.

The building was a plywood jail for Tom and Mike, and Sloan couldn't figure out what had happened. Why had Winston and Victor been killed? Why were Tom and Mike prisoners?"

He watched the current of the river sweep through the lake, listened to the sounds of the rushing water.

"Patience. I must have patience," Sloan reflected. "But what do I do?"

The answer came back, "Nothing."

Then two of the men came out of the cabin and went down to the lake. One got in a boat and launched, waving farewell to the other. He headed back to search for Sloan.

As the man traversed the lake, Sloan watched him carefully. In his binoculars he could clearly see that it was the man who shot Winston. He was being hunted again. They would not give up their pursuit.

The man entered their cabin and, after a few minutes, came out and started working his way down the shore in the boat. He headed, once again, toward the trapper's cabin.

Sloan followed the stranger until the boat disappeared into a small cove nearby. He could no longer hear the engine. Where did his pursuer go? He steadily observed the shore, and the trail behind him, turning his head often to cover both directions.

He glanced back at the trail, and thought he saw a shadowy figure run behind a tree. Then he heard a noise from behind.

"I'm hearing things," he said to himself.

Suddenly, the shadow of a man overwhelmed his own. Still on his knees, Sloan froze in fear. Sloan turned to face his adversary.

The barrel of a shotgun, his shotgun, was pointed downward in front of his face.

A ghostly figure loomed over him. The light of the moon outlined the figure. Sloan raised his hands and lowered his head in surrender. He was overcome with fear.

"You should be more careful about where you leave your weapon," whispered the voice.

He stared up in shock. "My God. I thought you were dead."

"Not yet," said the man quietly, as he extended his hand to help Sloan up.

It was Winston.

"What do you see," whispered the guide.

"What happened to you? You were shot in the head."

Moonshadows

"I'll tell you later. What have you seen across the lake?"

"They took everyone prisoner, and shot Victor. Victor is dead. I saw them carry his body out of the cabin and throw it in the lake," murmured Sloan. "Another man is nearby, along this shore, in a boat."

"We've got to find out what's going on," said Winston softly. "Every minute we wait puts our friends in more danger. How long have you been here?"

"A few hours, I really don't know how long. So much has happened. I thought they might know about this place."

"Tell me more," said Winston.

"That's all I know. They are obviously hunting for me. Why did they shoot you? What happened?"

"They're terrorists."

"Terrorists?"

"They wouldn't let us use the plane because they need it," said Winston.

"Then it's up to us," Sloan said, feeling more at ease now. His confidence was coming back. He felt stronger with a companion.

"Do you have another weapon?" Winston said.

"I've got a can of grizzly spray."

"Does that stuff really work?"

"Yes. I've used it in Alaska."

"OK," said Winston. "We must make a plan."

Robert B. Gregg

Chapter 29

They heard the boat motor again and went outside. They saw Ahmad right below them, motoring along and gazing their way. They knelt behind the brush and fell silent.

Ahmad continued his hunt. They glimpse him in the moonlight, but he cannot spot them as they hide in the gloom of the forest. Before reaching the rapids, Ahmad returns to the other side of the lake.

Sloan and Winston stand in the dark under the trees.

"They shot you, and you fell from the boat, and…"

"The bullet grazed my forehead, Winston said, pointing to the large gash covered in dried blood just over his eyes. " I bled like crazy. The shock knocked me into the water."

"I thought you were dead for sure," said Sloan, examining Winston's head. "What then?"

"I went straight down in the water and rolled along the sandy bottom," he said. "I swam down to the grassy island across from camp. I slid out on my belly into the reeds and waited for dusk. I swam across to the cabin using a log as flotation. The current is too strong to swim without help. I ended up a ways downstream and hiked the shore to get back to camp."

"What if they caught you?"

"They thought I was dead. The current is too strong to row there. They would have to use the engine to get across and I would hear them and hide. They would never find me. They cannot outfox me here. This is my domain."

Winston seemed angry and, at the same time, self-assured. His confidence rubbed off on Sloan. Tonight they would use the very darkness that Sloan feared.

"What you cannot see, you cannot deal with," Winston told Sloan. "We need the cover of night to do what must be done."

The forest was in constant motion from the wind, and the moon glow caused the shadows of the trees to dance along the ground. It was an eerie night, a night of dread.

The temperature dropped steadily. They fixed their eyes on their goal across the water. They were safe here for now, but they remained aware of their dire circumstance. They were out-manned and out-gunned. A near impossible task stood before them.

Sloan and Winston went inside the trapper cabin. They ate some food and drank a beer. Sloan had never seen Winston drink before. They talked about the plan. It must be perfect or they would all die.

There could be no mistakes. But mistakes do happen.

Chapter 30

"What is your problem, my brother? The Koran says if one attacks you, you may attack him in a like manner," said Fouad. "Their president attacked ISIL. We have the right to kill them as they kill us."

"They should not even be our prisoners," answered Joseph. "These men did not attack us."

"I know Allah's law!" Fouad shouted at Joseph. "Do not talk to me about things you do not understand. You embarrass me among these foreigners."

"What do you expect to accomplish by assassinating the President?" I asked.

"Much. We will strike fear in you, and you will realize we can extinguish evil wherever and whenever we want," said Fouad. "You are the great Satan. You abuse our people and lack morality. Look at your television, your movies. They are immoral by even Christian standards."

"I've read parts of the Koran," said Tom, "Why do you continue to kill those the Koran considers innocents?"

This statement by Tom irritated Fouad and he turned and stood over Tom, leaning his face into Tom's. "You know nothing! You are not innocents. Do not quote the Koran to me again or I will kill you."

Tom turned his head away from Fouad and gazed down at the floor. "That's better," said Fouad. "I need no more of this nonsense. I must ready the plane for my mission."

The situation overwhelmed me. My mind played a thousand scenarios and none of them had a good outcome. I lifted my head.

"Do not stare at me," Fouad said to me.

"I was not staring at you."

My reply did not set well with Fouad and he pulled his revolver out of its holster. I thought this was the end. I would die like Victor, simply shot, at will, by a religious fanatic.

Fouad turned and struck me a hard blow across the jaw with the gun butt. The chair I was tied to spun to one side and fell to the floor. My head hit against the plywood. Pain came instantly. My head throbbed. I could feel the blood trickling down my chin and neck. I needed some inner strength. I prayed for courage.

"We Wahhabis will someday lead the Muslim world to greatness," Fouad said. "It starts with work such as this. Your leaders must be eliminated. We must kill your Christian President."

"You are nothing but a paranoid religious zealot," Tom yelled at him.

Fouad hit Tom in the face with his clinched fist. Tom toppled over backward to the floor, and lay on his side, blood flowing from his lips and nose. He was dazed.

"That is being zealous," Fouad pronounced.

Joseph walked over and lifted Tom and his chair back to an upright position, then did the same for me.

Fouad went to the stove and poured himself more tea. A momentary calm came over the cabin.

Abraham and Ahmad were outside standing guard.

"I still do not understand," said Joseph to Fouad.

"Come to your senses, Joseph," said Fouad. "What we are doing is just. It is Jihad. Do not let these foreigners fool you with their talk."

Tom stared at me. He was still disoriented. In his eyes, all was lost.

"We still should not kill them," Joseph said, pleading for our lives.

"Speak to me no more about this."

"Even if they are prisoners of war we cannot kill them or harm them," Joseph said.

"You are too soft, my brother."

"I only speak the words of the Prophet."

"Where is this Sloan?" Fouad said to Tom and me, ignoring his brother. "He has either abandoned you both for the sake of himself or is, right now, instigating some plan of rescue."

Fouad walked over and opened the door.

"Ahmad, Abraham, come in here."

The two guards entered the cabin. "Watch these men. If they move at all, shoot them."

Fouad faced Joseph. "Do I not love you, Joseph? You are my brother. Let us not argue. This is our last evening together."

Without answering, Joseph walked out slamming the door behind him. Fouad stared at the door, then went to the table and sat down. The terrorists seemed tense. Abraham went outside and followed Joseph down to the lake.

"You are naïve, Joseph," Abraham said.

Moonshadows

Joseph didn't answer, but stood looking down at his feet.

Inside the cabin Ahmad said to Fouad, "Get some sleep. I will watch these infidels." Without a word, Fouad lay down and in seconds was deep in slumber.

Darkness engulfed the outside of the cabin. Only a Coleman lantern burned low inside and gave little light, casting eerie shadows everywhere.

My mind was haunted by the evil around me. The pain in my head was excruciating. I turned to Tom. He was slumped in his chair, exhausted, bloodied and asleep.

I tried to get some rest, nodding off here and there, awakening every time the cabin door squeaked with the changing of the guard. The pain and the captivity heightened my senses. I finally dozed off from sheer exhaustion and I awoke when Joseph entered the cabin. I glanced at him and our eyes met. He came close to me. "Do not speak," he whispered. "Your life is at stake."

I fell asleep again. I dreamed a horrible dream.

Tom and I slept steadily in our awkward positions until Ahmad slapping our faces abruptly awakened us.

"Wake up insolent mongrels," he said.

Reality was far worse than my dream. "My arms and neck ache, and my head throbs. Could I stand and stretch?" I asked. "The pain is bad."

"What do I care about your pain," said Ahmad. "You would not care about mine."

Fouad awakened to the rant.

Ahmad's frenzied gestures showed the rage he felt for us. He paused in his anger and asked us again. "Where is this Sloan?"

"I don't know," I answered. "We left him at the cabin. You understand as much as we do."

The lantern's light flickered.

"Joseph," Fouad ordered. "Pump some air into the lantern, and when you're finished, go outside and stand guard. Send Abrahim in. We must make the final plans."

Joseph pulled the lantern down off the nail in the rafter, and the light brightened when pumped. He hung it back up and quietly left.

Abrahim entered. The three men sat down at the table.

"The United States," said Fouad, facing the others across the table and still preaching to the choir. "They are Satan and abuse our people. They lack all morality and law." Ahmad and Abrahim nodded approval.

"They bring with them nothing but tyranny. They fight enemies whom they created in Afghanistan, in Iraq and in what they call the axis of evil. Their leaders must be eliminated."

Tom and I listened intently. They knew we were awake, but didn't care. My body quivered at the thought of our doom.

He lowered his voice, as if telling a secret. "We will leave in the morning. Early enough to put us in Ottawa in time for your president's speech."

"I pray to Allah," said Ahmad, "that Muslim rulers will awaken from their lethargy that has gone on since the signing of the peace agreement between Egypt and Israel."

I was tempted to speak out, but held back in fear.

"Today is a grave day," said Tom to the men. "When people who believe in God cannot have dialogue. We do you no harm. We are only fishermen."

"So you want to live, do you? Live with us in peace?" Ahmad said. "I find this an impossible thought."

As Ahmad spoke he inspected us with his hawk-like eyes.

It occurred to me there was no way to debate or discuss anything with these men that would not, eventually, lead to our deaths.

Fouad reminded me of a noble man who lost his way and found something to which he could devote his life. At first he seemed a tyrant, but I believe he was simply a crusader with perverted religious views.

"Our deaths, my brothers, will help lead Islam to victory," Fouad said to them. "Our faith will invade Europe and America, because the mission of Islam is to establish the caliphate."

"We will be the first of many," said Abrahim.

"We are marching to the battlefield," added Ahmad. "As we show the way, so many of our brothers will follow."

"Why?" Tom asked again.

"You are all enemies of Islam and the Arab homeland. You support the Zionists. You trade in the evil of the Arab countries who hold dialogue with you," said an angry Fouad. "The Saudi's and others will eventually pay the price of their corruption."

Moonshadows

"What you did in Paris and San Bernardino cannot be excused," I said. "How do you justify killing innocents?"

"They deserved what we did. We hate the French. The French are not innocent. They are useless whores," said Fouad. "They were among the first to describe the Hijab, or the veil as you call it, as offensive in nature. They outlawed the wearing of the veil. They do not understand the Hijab is a divine commandment, and if they did not understand this, they should ask. Our women must wear the veil.

Among the brothers in France are smart people who can stand against this vile stream in the war against wearing the veil. With Allah's help, our brothers in France will be able to handle this matter."

"Do you believe Allah wants you to kill innocent people?" Tom said.

"Yes. Our duty as brothers of the Jihad demands we kill," said Fouad.

"We are not evil," said Tom.

"You cannot look at yourselves and see the evil," said Fouad. "You cannot examine yourselves and understand what we perceive. The matter of America's attempt to take over the world is not new. Your country's tyranny is known by all. In the past, they fought secretly, and now they fight openly. No law in the world agrees to your occupation of Arab countries. Allah will help us. Had the Arab and Muslim countries been united, America and Israel could not withstand them."

"You will fail," Tom said boldly without fear.

"We will remain in power when you are long dead and gone," said Fouad.

Sloan was our last hope. He was somewhere out there in the wilderness. We had no doubt he would come, but when, and would he be in time to save us from these madmen?

Robert B. Gregg

Chapter 31

They could delay no longer. The time came to make a move. A full moon brightened a clear sky. A bitter cold wind blew down the river.

"I don't know if I can do this," Sloan said to Winston as they pulled the brush off the canoe that James hid near the shore the previous fall.

"We must succeed," said Winston. "I believe the harder we try, the more God will help us."

They stood facing one another. "My father once told me that you only get a few chances in life to stand tall," said the Cree. "He told me to never let those moments pass."

The terrorist camp beckoned them like a siren, luring them to an unknown destiny.

"You can't live every moment worrying about what might happen," Sloan thought. "Winston's right. It's time to face the phantoms of my mind."

They slipped the canoe down the bank and into the darkness.

A canoe is an ideal vehicle for the North. It will go where most boats will not, and it goes there quietly. The silence lets you get to fish before they know you are there. The fish have no suspicion, and that makes them easier to catch.

Tonight, they sought another kind of prey.

Sloan tossed his makeshift oar-crutch into the canoe and awkwardly boarded in the bow. The moonlight showed a determination and fear in both their faces.

"Our plan is good," Winston said softly, holding the canoe steady. "You and I are getting old. If we do not stop these men, we will grow old with regrets and have an emptiness to our lives."

"You're right," Sloan replied, with determination in his voice. He gazed across the water. They launched quickly and quietly. The men knew the difficulty facing them.

A faint light shone in the enemy's cabin. Each man had doubts as they paddled their way along the shore; they went upstream towards the rapids where the Albany came into the lake. They would cross, hidden by the waves and roar of whitewater.

Sloan hit hard, strong strokes in front. Winston paddled some, but spent most of his time steering against the current.

Sloan's thoughts jumped from his wife and children to murder and revenge. The current got stronger now; he gazed at the rapids ahead, paddling like a man possessed.

As they approached the roar of the fast-moving water, the moon came out from behind a cloud, and shadows danced with them in the boat as it bounced through the swift current. Sloan looked down at the dark moving shadows.

"They are Moonshadows," said Winston, pointing out the dancing figures. "Moonshadows are a good omen for my people."

They entered the heart of the rapids.

The river seemed louder than ever, the whitewater was a haunting picture in black and white. They crashed and tumbled in the moonlight. The current moved in small, uneven pulses.

They increased the tempo. Crossing whitewater in a canoe is always a tricky maneuver. The tumbling waves knocked them about and water splashed over the gunwale from both sides.

Still, they made their way steadily thanks to the brisk wind. As they neared the other shore the sounds of the rapids diminished and a peculiar silence encircled them.

Pulling up on a small spit of sand, they emptied the canoe of water, climbed in again and proceeded toward the stranger's cabin at a quick pace. Nearing the camp they got out of the canoe, and pushed it into some bushes on the bank.

Winston felt a pain in his head and became dizzy. He swayed, then staggered in the water.

"Are you all right?" Sloan said in a low voice, leaning on his crutch and steadying Winston.

"I'll be fine," said Winston regaining his senses. "Just a little woozy."

They were driven by impulse now. They waded the lake, staying as close to the shore as possible. They were on a mission.

"The time has come," whispered Winston. "We must move like ghosts, and remember, ghosts do not make noise."

Looking everywhere, they checked their surroundings. If they entered the forest here they would not be able to approach the cabin easily or quietly. The forest was dense, and the undergrowth impenetrable, especially at night.

"The woods are too thick," Winston whispered. "We will have to stay in the shallows until we get to the cabin. You go for the plane. I hope you're as good a demolition expert as you say."

Sloan just smiled confidently.

The guide put his right index finger to his lips in a sign of quiet. Sloan nodded approval. Years of wading trout streams taught Sloan how to move his feet silently in the water.

The moon outlined the cabin, with its windows of light. The approach would be easier, because they had the cover of night.

Stealthily they moved closer to the cabin where they observed two of the men standing outside, leaning on their rifles.

Step by step they progressed. Sloan and Winston sharply watched the shadows on the shore and in the woods. The wind moved the tree branches causing a constant crackling and rustling noise about them. They could hear every sound.

They paused. They heard voices inside the cabin engaging in a heated discussion. The guards no longer watched the shore. Their attention diverted to the argument inside.

Winston signaled for Sloan to wade across to the plane.

They separated. Winston went up into the forest toward the cabin. Sloan waded toward the plane.

Sloan had not gone far when his foot hit something and he stumbled, almost falling into the water and giving himself away.

He looked down in silence and at his feet in the moonlight was Victor's pale and spiritless face, lying just under the surface. A small burgundy hole was in his forehead. His desolate eyes stared up at Sloan in the haunting glow.

He brought himself under composure, reached down into the water, and closed Victor's eyes.

Robert B. Gregg

Chapter 32

As the shoreline brush cleared, Winston paused in the shadows, and kept a watchful eye on Sloan. The dizziness came again and he leaned against the tree to avoid falling. Exhausted, sleep would come easy, but not now, not here.

Sloan left his crutch on shore, and waded to the far side pontoon. He moved carefully knowing one sound would cause his death. The can of bear spray holstered on his belt gave him confidence, for he knew it would work.

He got the best of a charging mother bear with a blast in Alaska the year before.

"The spray stopped an angry grizzly," he thought. "A man shouldn't be a problem."

Winston held a double-barreled shotgun. Usually used as a bird gun for geese and ducks, he had added slugs to the load. A blast would blow a man's head off, if he got close enough.

With the guards distracted, Sloan ascended the short ladder and entered the plane. In the fuselage sat two cases of grenades, a bundle of plastic explosive and a 55-gallon drum of aviation fuel.

A strange looking football-shaped device, with a small light, was bolted into the floor. It looked to Sloan like it might be a bomb. He could not move the device.

He cut the wire from the grenade case with the needle nose pliers he used for fishing, pried open the other case and removed one of the grenades. He wedged the grenade into the back of the instrument panel.

Sloan rigged the wire to the plane's steering stick. He secured the connection, and ran it to the pin in the grenade, wrapping the wire tightly around the pin loop.

Sloan was cold and wet, and all business. Hunched over, he made his way back to the door, and waited for the guards to be distracted again so he might climb down the ladder and escape into the water unseen.

Through a small side window, Winston watched Ahmad and Abrahim as they talked in Arabic. He didn't understand what they said. Winston minded the men and also kept an eye on the plane.

After several minutes, he noticed Sloan move ashore, pick up his crutch and enter the woods east of the cabin, hiding in the shadow of the forest not far from the door.

Winston made his own way through the trees on the other side, almost falling down. They both stopped and rested.

The wind made a whistling sound as it tossed the upper branches of the spruce and jack pine surrounding the cabin. The moon drifted behind the clouds and again it grew dark.

The breeze died down and all went silent.

Sloan heard his heart pounding in his chest. A lone wolf howled in the night.

"What the hell are you doing here?" Sloan asked himself. "You're no hero."

Sloan knew what to do. Only courage could save him and the others.

They hid in the shadows of the gloomy forest like a pair of wolves waiting for a deer. Fear took over, but the need for vengeance remained stronger than the fear.

The wind came back as quickly as it had left; only this time with a pelting rain. It swirled down the lake and whipped the tree branches, sending small limbs down on the cabin roof.

The two guards took refuge inside.

Chapter 33

"What's going on?" Fouad said.

"A storm. A terrible storm," said Ahmad.

"Maybe Allah does not want us to kill these men," said an anguished Joseph alluding to Tom and me.

"I'm tired of your sympathy for these infidels," Fouad said to his brother. "Speak like that again and I will kill you myself."

Ahmad and Abrahim smiled their approval to the threat. They had tired of Joseph's whining.

"I'm not afraid of any storm," said Fouad, quickly striding to the cabin door. "Nothing can stop me now," and he dashed out into the storm.

Winston and Sloan watched him intently from the darkness.

The wind increased and the rain fell in sheets, fast and furious around them. Drenched and chilled to the bone, they shivered as they watched Fouad run down to the lake and test the plane's two tie-down lines.

Fouad gazed around, and up into the sky. The moon and stars had disappeared behind the clouds. The night turned black. The only light was a steady glow from the windows. He shook his head in disappointment, and walked back to the cabin.

Their weapons ready, they watched and listened to the terrorists inside.

"The tempest will not continue long," Fouad said entering the cabin. "For the winds comes too swift and swift storms do not last."

Ahmad and Abrahim nodded in agreement.

"You kill indiscriminately, many innocent people will die. How do you justify this?" Tom asked Fouad.

"I do not have to justify anything. We cannot win at your game, so we create our own rules."

"Why Ottawa?" I asked.

"They are careless about security. The Canadians rely on the Americans to protect them. They are fools," said Fouad.

"Terrorism, as you call our Jihad, is not a game or a war. It is Jihad! And Jihad is not a clean thing. We bring Holy War upon you like a disease."

"Then we will eradicate the disease," said Tom.

"Our people have nothing," he said, "but you and the Jews of Israel will not share the wealth."

"You talk like a communist," said Tom. "You use your religion as a framework for your evil terror."

"I don't have to listen to this any more," said Fouad. "Tape their mouths shut!"

The other men ripped some duct tape off the rolls and promptly silenced us.

"Get ready, Joseph," said Fouad. "Let us burn anything that will give them a clue as to how we planned this attack."

"I will not burn anything and I will not go!" Joseph said in defiance. "What you do is wrong."

"That is enough. You are a traitor!" Ahmad shouted. "You have never believed in our cause. Why did you come?"

Before Joseph answered, his brother came to his defense in a strange sort of way.

"I brought him along because I couldn't trust him," said Fouad. "I thought he would tell the authorities. What would you have me do, kill my own brother?"

"Yes," answered Ahmad instantly. "I would kill my own brother. What seems to be your problem?"

"I have no problem," said Fouad.

Time seemed short for Tom and me. Chaos surrounded us. Evil men quarreled about life and death. And they had little regard for us.

"Show your leadership and kill him," said Ahmad.

"You are a disgrace to our belief," said a scared Joseph to Ahmad. "Your hatred overcomes your good sense. Allah is always merciful."

"I've listened to enough of this talk. You, and Muslims like you, are the biggest enemies we have. I will give you mercy," said Ahmad as he pulled his gun out and quickly fired a round into Joseph's chest.

Joseph's eyes opened wide in surprise. He slumped to the floor on his knees, and fell on his side, blood pouring over the hand he held tightly to his gaping wound.

"Why?" Joseph said, looking up at Ahmad.

"Because your brother could not."

Fouad stepped toward Ahmad in anger, his hand on his weapon, but

Abraham stopped him.

"Let your displeasure end here," Abraham said.

Fouad knelt down and look at Joseph. For a moment concern came to his face.

"Why did you bring me here?" Joseph said. "Why are we killing people?"

"We have no choice my brother. You gave Ahmad no choice."

Fouad left Joseph curled up on the floor in mortal pain. He stood and gazed down at his brother.

"You have caused your own death. May Allah forgive you."

"Forgive me?"

"I'm glad to see you have come back to reality," said Ahmad to Fouad.

I glanced at Tom, knowing we came next. I sat pondering what I might do. In a matter of hours they would kill the U.S. President in Ottawa. Where was Sloan?

I twisted my hands and ankles against the tape. Nothing budged. The chair creaked.

Ahmad glanced at the sound. I stopped struggling. As soon as he looked away, I pulled and pried my hands until the skin under the tape turned raw and bled. I still made no progress.

"What do you think this is? A movie?" Ahmad said, catching me attempting to escape my bonds. "You aren't going anywhere."

Outside, Winston and Sloan overheard the shot and rushed, one on each side, to the front corners of the cabin. Winston carried the shotgun. Sloan took out the bear spray. They listened to the conversation through the plywood wall.

"Let us kill them now," said Ahmad. "They are of no use. The other man will not come. He is a coward."

"How can we shoot one of our own and let these men live?" Abraham said, pointing to Tom and me.

Fouad paced the room for a few seconds. He seemed in deep thought.

Joseph moaned in deep pain and writhed on the floor, a pool of blood slowly spreading from his wound.

Ahmad and Abraham waited for Fouad's approval.

"Take them outside and kill them," Fouad said, standing casually in the corner. Fouad knelt down again next to his writhing brother. The other two began untying Tom and me for our final walk.

Fouad did not speak to Joseph. He simply stared at him and drawing his pistol, put it against Joseph's temple and fired. Perhaps the only mercy Fouad could find, but enough for Joseph.

"Sleep well my brother," he softly said.

The duct tape gave them problems moving us, and finally, in frustration, Ahmad and Abrahim drew their knives and hastily cut the tape from our legs. Our hands were still bound. Ahmad grabbed me and Abrahim took Tom. They walked us to the door.

"Farewell Infidels. Maybe, in death, you will go to the Happy Hunting Ground and join your Indian friend," said Fouad, smiling as we passed him.

The door opened. The four of us went into the storm.

As we stepped off the porch, Winston leveled his shotgun at Abrahim and fired. The slug opened a gaping, fatal wound in Abrahim's chest and he was blasted backward against the cabin wall, as Tom rolled onto the grass unharmed. At that very moment, Sloan ran up and emptied the can of bear spray into Ahmad's face, also nailing me in the process.

The spray blinded Ahmad. He released me and put his hands to his face. I fell to the ground. My eyes and nose stung and burned. Tears flowed. I rolled away as far as I could, and came to rest against a tree.

Ahmad struggled to see, while pulling his revolver from the holster.

Hearing the shotgun blast, Fouad ran from the cabin and, seeing the situation, dashed for the plane.

Ahmad, holding one hand over his eyes, began randomly firing the pistol while stumbling and staggering.

Sloan lifted me up and we got behind a tree as Ahmad fired toward the lake. Soon, a clicking sound signified an empty weapon.

Ahmad kept pulling the trigger as he spun around facing the cabin. Then Winston, cool and calm, walked up behind him and placing his shotgun barrel next to Ahmad's head, ... fired!

Pieces of Ahmad's brains and skull splattered against the wet cabin wall.

"Who is going to the Happy Hunting Grounds now?" Winston said sternly to the lifeless body collapsing to the ground.

"Fouad," yelled Tom. "He's gone to the plane!!"

Fouad untied the two ropes, jumped onto the pontoon and climbed into the pilot's seat and started the engine.

Winston dashed toward the plane in the pouring rain. The wind blew hard into his face as he struggled to run and reload at the same time.

Tom staggered to his feet and awkwardly rushed to the lake, his hands still tied behind his back.

Sloan stayed, helping me to my feet.

Winston fumbled with the gun, still trying to reload, while Fouad set the flaps and taxied to the center of the lake. He had escaped.

We stood frustrated on the shore, watching the plane taxi away.

Fouad would complete his plan. We saw his face in the cockpit light, filled with triumph. He glanced at the men on shore, outlined by the faint light coming from the open cabin door. We couldn't stop him.

The terrorist act would happen. The President would die. No one would stop him. Losing his men didn't matter. They were going to die any way.

He checked his gauges. He adjusted the flaps. The plane sped across the water carrying Fouad towards his goal of assassination. As the plane achieved takeoff speed, Fouad pulled back the steering stick. The plane left the water and lifted into the air.

Fouad pulled the stick back a little more so the plane could clear the trees at the end of the lake. Suddenly, he felt an unusual pressure, and something pinged against the metal console. He glanced down and saw a ring.

He recognized it immediately. He had used grenades when he fought for the Mujahedin in Afghanistan.

Inside the grenade, the striker hammered down on the percussion cap. The impact ignited the cap and the fuse had started.

Fouad reached under the dash and grabbed the grenade, pulling it away from its lodged position. He knew the slow-burning material inside took four seconds to burn through.

He smiled briefly as he held the grenade up to throw it out of the window; then the detonator fired, initiating a series of blasts that lit the night sky.

We stood like statues in awe and astonishment as the plane

disintegrated in a huge fireball over the lake in front of us. Burning orange fragments fell from the sky and then all turned black again.

"Did you think he would get away?" Sloan said to us as he casually leaned on his broken oar.

We turned and gazed at him in stunned silence.

"After all, I was once a demolition man," he said nonchalantly

Chapter 34

The nightmare had ended. Back at the cabin, exhaustion set in, and we all slept well.

The sun rose on "check flight day" with a beautiful golden light against a pure blue horizon.

I got up and checked my watch. Just past seven. My eyes still watered a little from the bear spray. Everyone else still slept. I smiled to myself.

I had prepared the coffee pot the night before. I lit the burner under the pot, and fired up the stove, turning the flame on high. The burner came on creating neon blue warmth.

"For crying out loud," I thought. "I'll light them all. We'll get the morning chill out of here faster than the wood stove can do it." I turned on all four burners. It seemed a good idea.

"To hell with the propane," I thought, "we deserved some comfort after what we had been through. I stoked the wood stove and got a roaring fire going.

Tom woke and struggled out of his sleeping bag.

"I feel like a new man," he said, and started doing his stretches as the coffee began percolating.

The cabin filled with the yellow-orange glow of the sun.

"Coffee's ready," I said. "How many glugs?"

"Just two. I want to be sober when Ray arrives."

I poured two cups of coffee and added the Bailey's to both. I stood by the propane stove. Tom sat at the table.

"Here's to survival," I said, toasting with my cup.

"Here's to fellowship," said Tom, raising his mug.

"When do you think we should start making the circles in the lake with the boat?" I asked.

"Well, Ray's a pretty punctual guy and he said noon. I think we're safe if we start around 11:30."

Winston was the next to rise. He got up, smiled and held out his cup. I poured. "What's for breakfast?"

"What do you want? Since we're leaving early, we have quite a bit of food left."

"Anything. I'm just glad we're having breakfast."

"We've got a lot of bread left over. How about some of Charlie's famous cinnamon and nutmeg French toast?" I said.

"Sounds good," came the half-awake answer from Sloan as he inched out of his sleeping bag.

We were alive and well. The four of us sat around the table, ate our breakfast and drank coffee without much being said.

Sloan limped outside with his mug in hand and stood facing the morning sun, watching the flow of the river. He never said a word during breakfast.

"He's acting a little strange," I said to Tom and Winston.

"I think not," said Winston. "He has acted like a man, and sometimes that alone is a rare and strange thing."

Winston went outside and placed himself next to Sloan. Tom and I went out, and stood on the porch.

"Well Sloan," Winston said, "how are you doing today?"

Sloan turned and looked at Winston with tears in his eyes.

"My good friend," he said. "I wouldn't be here, if you hadn't showed me the way."

"We've traveled far together Sloan. Things did appear bad didn't they?"

"They sure did," he answered. They stared out at the sun rising on the horizon.

"I'm still tired," said Sloan, laying down his crutch and sitting on porch steps in front of us. Winston sat down at his side.

"Next year I'll take you to a spot where the biggest brook trout in this river live," said Winston.

Sloan scratched at the dirt with a stick. "I'd like that," he said and put his hand on Winston's shoulder. "I'm going to hold you to your commitment."

"You can count on it," said Winston. "A promise is something that lasts until completed. There's no going back."

Chapter 35

The bright sun settled high above now. Small, fleecy clouds drifted across the spring sky.

The clock showed near noon. Ray would be due soon for the check flight. The weather was clear. No reason he wouldn't come. However, several years earlier the pilot failed to arrive for two additional days, because he had to fly firefighters to a forest fire.

Sloan and I gazed out of the window into the morning sun watching Winston and Tom. After recovering Victor's body, they followed one another, drawing a circle of waves on the lake with their boats.

Our two companions were dead. The river killed Charlie. Victor was brutally murdered.

The terrorists? Well, they simply got what they deserved.

"Do you hear that?" Sloan said.

"No."

"Listen closely. How about now?"

A sound, ever so faint, could be heard. Not sure at first, we went outside, and it was clearly the distant humming of a plane, and then Ray's bright orange DeHavilland Otter appeared on the horizon in front of us.

"It's Ray!!" Sloan joyfully shouted. "It's Ray!"

The plane flew in low over the canopy of spruce trees on the opposite shore, and came toward us. Winston and Tom continued to circle in their boats with one arm steering and the other waving at the plane.

The sun flashed off the glistening plane as Ray tilted the wings over the lake. He started his approach. The plane made a turn and came in from the east, preparing to land. Tom and Winston raced back to shore.

"Looks like we're out of here," said Sloan.

"We've made it, Sloan."

"Yea!"

I turned and faced him. "What's wrong?" Sloan said.

"Nothing."

"I've accomplished a lot in my life, but nothing heroic," I told him. "You should be proud of what you've done. You and Winston saved us."

"I was just surviving like you," Sloan answered. "I don't think of myself as a hero. Hell, if Winston hadn't come back from the dead I might have just hid in the woods until they left."

Robert B. Gregg

"I doubt that. What counts is you didn't go and hide. You risked your life to rescue us."

"You would have done the same for me," said Sloan.

"I don't know," I said.

"I believe you would and that's enough for me."

He put his arm around me and we watched the plane touch down. The spray flew from the pontoons as Ray powered down the Otter. He taxied to the far side, turned and headed our way motoring across the lake.

We saw his smiling face as he approached.

Tom and Winston pulled their boats up on shore, leaving the dock to Ray.

We would be stopping in Nakina to tell the authorities what happened.

We seldom realize how we will act when push comes to shove. We did our best, and deemed ourselves fortunate to have survived. I thought of Charlie and Victor.

The plane coasted toward the dock. We all arrived to greet it. Ray got out and stood on a pontoon smiling at us. He tossed the tie-down rope to Winston.

"So how's the fishing?" he asked.

THE END

Also available on Amazon.com, CreateSpace.com, Ingram, and Bookbub.com

King Arthur &
The Holy Grail

Robert B. Gregg

The Complete Grail Legend

Copyright © 2016   Robert B. Gregg   332 pages

ISBN-13: 978-1512136845 & ISBN-10: 1512136840

Avalon House Classics

Robert B. Gregg

Made in the USA
Charleston, SC
13 January 2017